The Urbana Free Library

To renew materials call
217-367-4057

As Good As Dead

As Good As Dead

Ralph McInerny

Five Star • Waterville, Maine

Five Star First Edition Mystery Series.

Published in 2002 in conjunction with Tekno-Books and Ed Gorman.

Set in 11 pt. Plantin by Elena Picard.

Printed in the United States on permanent paper.

Library of Congress Cataloging-in-Publication Data

McInerny, Ralph M.
    As good as dead / Ralph McInerny.
       p. cm.—(Five Star first edition mystery series)
    ISBN 0-7862-4179-9 (hc : alk. paper)
    1. South Bend (Ind.)—Fiction. 2. Murder for hire—
Fiction. I. Title. II. Series.
PS3563.A31166 A93 2002
813'.54—dc21   2002025191

For Jody Bottum

One

Crowe took the South Shore from Chicago because it was an anonymous way to travel. The train terminated at the airport. Crowe waited for the others to get off, but he did not wait too long. When he came down the steps onto the platform an embracing couple broke up and walked away hand in hand. To his left, there was a small parking lot for those meeting the train. Across a service road was the much larger lot for airport patrons, short term and long term. Crowe crossed the street swiftly and moved into the sea of cars toward long-term parking.

Flashy powerful cars did not attract him, reds or whites or those with sunroofs, expensive models. They were not what he needed. He stopped by a dusty sedan, made sure the parking ticket was in it, and went to work on the door. It took several minutes before he had opened it, popped the hood and gone around to the front of the car.

"Something wrong?"

The voice came from behind him. Crowe did not turn. He had the wire in his hand. He moved his arm closer to his chest and felt the hard resistance of his weapon. He turned slowly, a neutral expression on his wide flat face. It was a kid, androgynous, wearing a ponytail and one earring.

"Can I help you?"

Crowe looked at him. "You know how to steal cars?"

One side of the kid's mouth went up, making the opposite

eye close. "Lose your key?"

"In movies, people just open the hood and do something . . ."

"I'll show you."

Crowe stepped back and let the ponytail take his place. The kid bent over the engine. It was a shame, him being so helpful and all. Crowe waited until the engine roared into life and, when the kid stepped back, brought the butt of the gun solidly down on the back of his head. He moved forward to get his hands under the kid's arms before he fell, pulling the now inert body away from the car. He eased him onto pavement damp from the misty rain.

Before he got behind the wheel of the car, Crowe looked around. The train in which he had come stood motionless, its bright windows empty. The last car was pulling out from the railroad parking lot. Then Crowe noticed the girl.

He knew right away she was a girl, although she could have been the twin of the kid he'd just whacked on the head. She was maybe fifty yards away, with four double rows of cars between them, but their eyes met and even across that distance Crowe could tell that she had watched what he had done to the pony-tailed kid. Her friend?

"Larry?" she called.

Her voice came thinly over the roofs of the cars, rising into a plaintiff question. Leaning on the open door of the car whose engine was running, Crowe decided she had to go. The ponytail had spelled trouble, but the girl was more dangerous. The boy would have remembered the man in the black topcoat in the parking lot, but would he have wanted to say he had just hot-wired a car for him? The girl was different. She had seen him clobber the kid.

Crowe looked at the body, face down on the damp mottled blacktop and was sure that no matter how long he stared there would be no movement indicating breathing. When he looked up again the girl was gone.

This was a definite problem. Crowe got behind the wheel, to get out of the rain, to think, to get moving. But just sitting there was not the thing to do.

He backed up, glanced at the inert body of the Good Samaritan and shot down an aisle toward the exit flanked by pay shacks. The girl could be back there, hiding behind the cars, waiting. Now she would go to where the boy was. A definite problem.

There was an empty space at the end of the row, and he began to brake but then thought better of it. He continued on to the pay shack, rolled down his window and handed his ticket to the attendant. The shack was the size of a phone booth, the woman attendant had a radio going full blast, a radio talk show. She frowned at his ticket, chewed on her lower lip, hit the keys of her cash register. The amount that flashed at him suggested the owner of the car had been away for days.

"You need a receipt?"

Crowe was certain now he should have ditched the car and come up with an alternative plan. The simple idea—to come down here from Chicago by train, steal a car and keep his appointment—was unraveling. He had forty-five minutes before he met with the woman who called herself Mrs. Lewis. Plenty of time if things had gone right, more than enough time. He was beginning to feel pressured.

"No thanks," he called to the attendant, keeping out of sight.

The barrier lifted, and he moved forward. Ahead the road stretched invitingly to the highway where a semaphore glowed through the dove grey twilight. Why not just press down on the gas and get the hell out of here?

A less methodical man would have succumbed to that impulse. But Crowe prided himself on doing things right. When he was on assignment it was important that he become an invisible man, leaving no trace. The past ten minutes had been atypical. In his head, planning, he tried to imagine every contingency, plausible and implausible, and deal with it in advance. But he had not imagined a kid coming up behind him and offering to start the car for him. He had not imagined being observed when he took the car, let alone when he hit the kid over the head. But he had been, and now that girl was back there in the lot and he could not just drive away.

Twenty yards past the pay shack a road swung off to the left, leading back to the air terminal. Crowe took it, driving deliberately and carefully, and turned into short-term parking.

His eye had raked the parking lot as he circled back to it, but he had not seen the girl. She was there, he was sure of it. Perhaps she was already creeping toward her fallen friend. Any minute now, she might sound the alarm.

He parked the car, got out and moved swiftly toward the terminal building. He pushed through the revolving doors and into the busy interior where people hurried this way and that, long lines of waiting passengers twisted toward counters where attendants with frozen smiles checked baggage and assigned seats. Crowe had half a mind to catch a feeder back to Chicago and write this whole day off as a mistake. He would be out some money, but it was a small sum, a paltry sum, compared with what the trouble in the lot could develop into.

He took the stairs to the observation level two at a time, but the window he wanted was on the landing. It overlooked the parking lot. Half a minute after he took up his post, he saw her.

She might have been standing where he had last seen her. Had she watched him leave the lot? Had she watched him come around to short-term parking in front of the terminal? He had the uncanny feeling that she was looking at him now. The interior light on the window and the misty rain outside made it easy to imagine that once more their eyes were meeting. He pressed his cheek against the glass and shaded his eyes. If she was looking at him, if she'd seen him re-park the car and enter the terminal, he had nothing to lose.

His shaded eyes grew more accustomed to the lack of light outside. The girl stood next to a car with her hand resting on its front fender; she was turned toward the terminal, her head was lifted and there was no mistake about it—she was looking directly at him.

Crowe stepped back. He went down the stairs and moved indecisively past restrooms, a gift shop, a candy store from which the smell of popcorn emanated. The building formed a great curving arc, with the interurban train depot at one end, then all the airline counters and, at the far end, a bus depot. Crowe quickened his step. He was going to abort this job, that was for goddam sure. He would hop a bus out of here, go wherever it was going, get away from that girl. The slim watching figure standing out there in the light rain filled him with apprehension.

A middle-aged misshapen couple stood side by side at the bus counter, saying in high stupid voices that they had to get to Indianapolis.

"The bus to Indianapolis left at two o'clock," the clerk said.

"Isn't there another one?"

"Sure."

"When?"

"Two o'clock."

"Two in the morning?"

"Two tomorrow."

Crowe sat down. He thought of what he was doing. He had come to South Bend to meet a woman who had identified herself as Mrs. Lewis. She had been Mrs. Brown at the beginning, but he ran her through the usual steps and she confessed she wasn't Mrs. Brown, she was Mrs. Lewis. That was a lie too, he had checked her out by that time, but he let it go. It was important for the client to talk, just talk, in order to pretend they weren't really discussing what they were discussing. Eventually this client would be good for a lot more than the price he was asking, Crowe knew that. His situation at the moment made this important knowledge. He could not afford to turn tail and run away from the prospect of that kind of money. And all because of some frail girl standing out there in the rain. He made a noise of disgust.

Someone took the seat beside him. He glanced over and then twisted in his chair. It was the girl.

"Hi."

He just looked at her. Long straight hair, wet from the rain as if she had just stepped out of a shower. One eye seemed a little off and her glasses had slipped from the bridge of her nose. She started to smile and then thought better of it.

"His name was Larry."

Crowe still said nothing. He could sweep this kid away with one arm; she couldn't weigh much more than a hundred ten. She looked like a half-drowned cat in out of the rain, but she spelled big trouble.

"I met him on the South Shore. He said he had a car in the lot. I saw him attack you."

"Attack me?"

"If you hadn't turned around he would have. He told me

all kinds of things coming down from Chicago. I know he meant to steal a car."

She pushed her glasses up on her nose and turned toward the counter where the overweight couple that wanted to go to Indianapolis were protesting loudly. The mouth of the girl beside him was slightly open and little rabbit teeth were visible. There was nothing attractive about her. She was no better than the Larry she was willing to forget all about now. She wanted a companion, someone to look after her, someone to be with, at least for a while. That seemed to be the deal.

She said, "Did you call the police?"

"Come on."

He stood up but she did not. She pressed back into the seat, looking up at him. "I didn't have anything to do with it."

"Let's go."

"To the police?"

He shook his head. "To the parking lot. I want to steal a car."

Two

Lucy Flood's life was divided into two lopsided parts, the forty-one years prior to a week ago last Monday and the eleven days since. On the other side of the line was the stranger she had been, an attractive woman, healthy, who still did not think of herself as middle-aged. Because she wasn't. She was young! She looked it, she felt it, she acted it. Her days were filled with a dozen things. Everyone commented on her energy and her ability to become enthusiastic about so many things. People liked and admired her and way down deep inside Lucy approved of herself. She was what she wanted to be. And then had come the routine appointment with Lodge, to talk over the results of her tests.

She had wedged the visit into a full morning. She remembered so clearly saying to herself on the way up in the elevator, "This better not take too long."

Later she would imagine that even the receptionist had looked oddly at her when she first came in. The nurse who took her down the hall to an examination room put a hand under her elbow and spoke in the too-sweet tone reserved for the ill. Lodge did not look her in the eye when he came in. He closed the door, went to the little desk, sat and opened a folder. At the time, Lucy hardly noticed these things. Only afterward when she went through it minute by minute did she realize what had happened. At the time, she checked her watch against the clock on the wall.

"Your clock is slow."

"Is it?"

"Almost three minutes."

"Three minutes," Dr. Lodge repeated. He picked up a sheet from the open folder. He still had not looked directly at her. "I would have preferred your husband to be here for this."

"My husband!"

The words just flew from her mouth. It was ridiculous to speak of Warren being present when she was talking with her doctor. Warren was the main reason she kept so busy, as if by keeping up a breakneck pace she could always be three minutes or so ahead of the present. Dr. Lodge was looking at her now. And telling her the same thing.

If he were speaking Chinese or Magyar his tone would have been enough to convey the meaning of what he said. It was the tone rather than the words she heard anyway, the tone of a doctor giving seriously bad news to a patient. He used the technical term, carcinoma, not plain old cancer, which ironically was her zodiacal sign, as if her life had been lived under this threat from the beginning. She amazed herself by the calmness she displayed. He would have been justified in thinking that she had come here expecting to hear this.

"How long?"

"How long?" He emitted a kind of laugh. "The question is rather when to begin treatment."

"What kind of treatment?"

He seemed relieved to be able to launch into a little lecture. Some would advise surgery. He paused. He could not say they were wrong, not always, but his own philosophy was to avoid invasive surgery, to give chemotherapy a try, and radiation.

"I am relieved that you're taking this calmly. You are right

15

to do so. We can do much *much* more now than we could even a few years ago."

What they could now do was postpone the inevitable. Whether they cut into her or gave her potions that would make her hair fall out and dosed her with radiation, her life was over. That was the message of his tone, the dirge carried by his modulated voice which dropped almost to inaudibility at the end of sentences. But now his tone was changing; now he spoke as to a coconspirator, a woman who agreed to play the role of dutiful patient, following sensible orders to the grave.

"If you'd like to come back with your husband . . ."

"You recommend a second opinion?"

He frowned. "Only if you feel that you would feel . . ."

"I think I would."

He nodded, his lips a thin line. "Very well. I can give you some names."

"I have someone in mind. Doctor, is all this confidential?"

She had shocked him. "Yes. Of course."

"But others know."

"What others?"

"Your staff, the people at the lab."

"Confidentiality governs them all."

"I was sure it did."

But she was out of his good graces. What did the opinion of others matter anymore? Suddenly she felt that her life had always been governed by thousands of unseen witnesses, judging, appraising, by and large approving, as she had thought, but nonetheless her mentors. Who were they? Dr. Lodge? He sat, nervous, frowning, acting for all the world as if he had never before had to give a patient such news. Did he imagine that he himself was immune? Perhaps that is why people go into medicine, hoping to escape the common lot.

"I urge you not to overreact, Lucy. There was a time when we kept information like this from the patient, when there was so little that could be done. But now . . ."

His hand went out in a lazy arc, as if he were unable to gather in all that could be done for patients like herself. That was when Lucy became an observer of the scene, no longer the woman seated on the end of the examination table, attending to what her doctor said, but floating above and beyond as well, looking on, an observer. What she observed was no longer unique. The fate that awaited her awaited everyone born into this world. How could anyone be surprised at the most obvious thing about any of us, that we are all destined to die?

Lucy took it with her like a secret from Lodge's office. On the way to her car, she passed the First Church of Christ Scientist. Was there a second? Next to the church was a reading room. Susan stopped and stared unseeing at the window display, trying to imagine Christ in a lab coat, in pursuit of the hidden laws of the universe he had created. What did Christian Scientists believe? Did they reject medicine? Or was it only that they believed in a better medicine?

Did she? That morning, the day before, throughout her lifetime, she had always thought of herself as a Christian. She had been baptized. There were photographs of the event which had been passed on to her. Back in her car, behind the wheel, staring straight ahead, she thought of God and did not know if she believed in an unimaginably powerful and wise being who had willed everything out of nothingness and even now held it all in the palm of his hand. She waited for an inner click of assent, but it did not come.

Driving out of the clinic lot, she noticed how carefully she performed the task. She was a good driver, much better than Warren, though of course that was not something a wife said to her husband. Her life seemed a vast repertoire of survival skills. Of course. What else is life but a long doomed battle with death? She felt a calm unpanicky impulse to drive, just drive, and leave everything behind. She could get on the Interstate, turn East or West, what did it matter, and drive on out of her life.

Just as calmly, after turning it over carefully in her mind, she rejected the thought. She could drive all day and not drive away from herself; she would still be a forty-one-year-old woman who had just learned that she had a terminal disease. There was an hour before the meeting of the board of the Homeless Center, one of her charities that made Warren groan.

"Homeless," he snorted. "That makes it sound like a disease. Why not call them Foodless? It would come to the same thing. They are people who count on others to take care of them and want to make you feel guilty about it besides."

"I don't feel guilty."

"Oh, I don't mean you. You're an angel of mercy."

He professed to find her noble and altruistic. Perhaps that is how she saw herself. Above the fray, giving a little consolation to the poor wretches who stayed on and on at the Homeless Center. One day a month she visited prisoners. Not that she actually worked with them. Her talents were for administration. She was as smug as Warren.

Her memories of Warren, her husband of fourteen years, were snapshots of a stranger. Yesterday she would have said, in the improbable supposition that anyone had asked, that she loved him. She was his wife, wives love their husbands, what else? Now she wondered if she even liked him. She wondered too if he would miss her. She thought of Yolande, but shrugged off her annoyance.

The rest of her day was a sequence of sharply etched

scenes, one following the other, making no collective sense when she thought of them in the light of what she had been told in Dr. Lodge's examination room. No one who saw her that day or in subsequent days could have guessed that she had been radically changed by what Dr. Lodge had told her. Nothing could ever be the same again.

That night she and Warren dined with Max Kramer and his wife at the country club. Warren and Max had been golfing; Lucy and Yolande would join them at the club. A night like a dozen others, until Max began to speak of hired killers.

"That's a pretty risky transaction," Warren said authoritatively.

The men lighted cigars, as much out of defiance of the new Puritanical mood sweeping the country club as because they enjoyed them. Lucy watched Warren let the smoke roll uninhaled and untasted from his parted lips. Max smoked a cigar with the same concentration that he represented his clients and played golf.

Yolande said, "Just discussing such a matter with a supposed assassin could get you into trouble, couldn't it?"

"Adultery in the heart?" Warren asked, lifting his brows at Yolande. Lucy felt no twinge of anger or jealousy. The two of them thought to divert suspicion by openly flirting with one another. Now it seemed even sillier than it had.

"Oh, it's more serious than that, Warren. In the law, I mean."

Max told of several recent cases, right here in Indiana, where a spouse had been tried along with the hired assassin. As often as not such arrangements went wrong.

"They're the only ones we hear of, I suppose," Lucy said.

"Good point."

"How do people find killers like that?" Yolande wondered.

19

"They're not in the Yellow Pages," Max said.

"The prisons are full of them," Warren said.

Lucy thought of her monthly visits to the prison in Michigan City. Her original intention had been to teach illiterate inmates how to read, but that was a long-term project and she wanted instant gratification from the good works she performed. She offered to help inmates with their correspondence. That was how she had met Lorenzo, a savage killer whose correspondence was largely with women who had conceived a passion for him. The exchanges were remarkable for their explicitness and Lucy would have sought another way to help prisoners if she had not found such elemental expressions of animal lust hideously fascinating. Lorenzo had no alternative to such pornographic correspondence, but surely the women who wrote to him had other opportunities? Lorenzo shook his head at this suggestion.

"They're freaks. Missing a leg, an eye, ugly, something wrong with them."

Lucy protested, pointing to the photographs of his correspondents that Lorenzo always brought with him.

"You think those are really pictures of them?"

"Don't you?"

One photo, he said, was that of a young actress. He assumed the others too were masks behind which his women correspondents hid.

"Why not? It's just a game we're playing." His voice altered from a speaking tone to a species of singing. "You know that song?"

"Sing some more."

"Come on."

"Lorenzo, why are you here? What did you do?"

He looked at her. "I killed people."

"People? How many?"

He shrugged. "They said sixteen."

"Sixteen!"

"There were more."

"What had they done to you?"

"Nothing. I didn't even know them. They were all strangers."

He had done it for money. This was worse, far far worse, than his pornographic letters, but it was more fascinating too, in its grisly way. But he didn't like to talk about it.

"Not now. I'm in the mood for love." He was singing again. "But if you ever want a little help along those lines . . ." He completed the sentence with a slow wink.

That was the remark, along with its winking completion, that came back clearly and distinctly as Lucy sat at table in the Country Cub dining room with her husband and the Kramers on the evening of the day she had learned she was going to die.

Lorenzo put her in touch with Crowe.

Three

She'd been given the name Madeline by the grandfather who raised her.

"I thought my mother was my sister." Her smile was meant to show how dumb she used to be.

Crowe said, "Madeline's a nice name. Why don't you use it?"

"He always called me Paddelin."

"Why?"

She snuffled and hugged herself. Crowe wanted to give her his jacket to put around her bony, shivering body. "Some song he used to sing."

"Paddlin' Madeline home."

Her face lit up like a store window when she smiled. "That's it."

Her reaction, and his, settled what *they* were going to do, settled that they would do it, not just him. Crowe felt like the guy who's just guessed right on *Jeopardy* and is getting the applause; he felt wise, smart, looked up to. And he felt protective toward her. He wanted her warm and dry and out of the dim unkind lights of the terminal.

She told him that she and the kid lying out there in the parking lot had noticed him on the train. They were going to grab a car from the lot and that is why they were following him.

"Larry said to let you open her up and start it for us."

"Then what?"

"Go!" Her voice trembled with the adventure packed into that one sound.

"I'm sorry about him."

She held his eyes. "He wasn't my husband."

Husband! She didn't look old enough to have a husband. "I didn't say he was."

"He said we'd get married; that's why I went with him." Her smile started up, weakened, tried again and then died for good. "Not that I believed him."

Crowe felt good now about hitting the kid in the parking lot, as if he had been punishing him for taking this girl on a trip with no purpose but a chance to shack up in strange places until he tired of her and took off. Well, he was gone sooner than he planned.

"If you're going to Indianapolis, forget it."

It was the fat woman whose whining complaints he had been hating. She stood before Crowe and her brows lifted into her bangs. Her remark conferred an unfamiliar status on him. He was just a guy with his girl who wanted to catch a bus and was running into scheduling problems like everyone else.

"Take a motel room, he says." Her husband repeated the incredible suggestion in an imitation black voice that would have earned him a shiv at Michigan City or any of the other public institutions Crowe had graduated from. There were only two; three, if you counted the probation he'd been on as a minor.

"Here." The lady took a Kleenex from the big flat leather handbag whose short strap kept it tucked right under one of her fat arms and tight against her body. Madeline scrambled to her feet, grabbed the Kleenex and clamped it to her face. She hunched over, looking around at them with wide disappointed eyes. The sneeze that did not come. The fat lady tucked her handbag back under her arm and took hold of

Madeline. "There's a restroom."

And off they went. The man lowered himself into a seat, wheezing and creaking. He sat upright and began to massage his knee caps. "Goddam rain makes me ache."

Crowe nodded. A fierce debate was raging inside him. As soon as the girl disappeared through the john door with the fat lady he could have been on his feet and out of here. Whatever trouble she spelled was nothing compared to sitting here like some damned hick complaining about intercity bus service. The first thing he'd noticed was the schedule up on the wall, plain for anyone to see behind the counter. There wasn't a bus to Chicago until morning either. He wanted to feel superior to the complaining couple, but he was dumber than they were. This whole thing had developed into one improvisation after another. Had he ever in his most imaginative moments thought of getting back to Chicago by bus? No, and the reason was that buses weren't what they used to be. You didn't just buy a ticket and leave town a few minutes later. The plan had crashed, and it was cover your ass time.

But he didn't leave. As soon as he started talking with the girl she stopped being someone he had to worry about. She reminded him of someone, himself probably, before he'd realized that only brains and doing things right would keep him out of places like Michigan City or worse.

The restroom door opened and Madeline came out, spare, birdlike, as if she were in custody and the fat lady was a matron. She hurried toward him, followed by the waddling lady who spoke to Crowe.

"You get her into a warm bed, or she's going to have pneumonia."

Madeline held out her hand. Crowe didn't take it, but he stood. What had she told the fat lady in there?

"Check into a motel," her husband said, imitating the

24

man behind the counter again. He broke himself up. There were tears in his eyes, when he repeated it to Crowe. "Check your daughter into a motel."

"We's going home!" Madeline took his hand and tugged him toward the glass doors. Crowe watched their reflections as they approached, one medium sized man sure as hell not old enough to be this girl's father, heading hand in hand into the rainy night with no place to go. Outside, Madeline waved frantically and the lights of a cab went on. It rattled forward before Crowe had a say in the matter. She pulled him right into the back seat behind her. She was already talking to the driver.

"You don't want to do this, say so, but can you see that motel yonder?"

The driver groaned and put his clipboard back on the seat.

"I don't blame you, but we're stranded here and I'm catching cold and we don't want to spend the night sitting up in the terminal."

The driver was nodding resignedly before she finished. The car started forward. He didn't start the meter. The sound of the tires on the wet pavement, the row of lamps along the road on which Crowe might have gotten the hell out of here forty-five minutes ago, the scraping complaint of the wipers on the windshield, put Crowe in mind of something pretty, a poem, something that lifted your feelings. The girl was holding his hand tightly in her own and leaning against his arm on the holster side of his body.

"This rain gonna keep up?" she asked the driver.

"All night and into the morning."

"Ain't that good for business?"

"It is if you like driving welfare mamas around." He shook his head and seemed ready to give them the benefit of his thinking on the subject.

"And people who want to go a block?"

"Hey, what's the difference?" He turned his head, keeping his eyes on the road. "That motel's not much of a place."

"Is it warm and dry?"

"There's a better one not too far away."

Crowe guessed that the guy would like to do them an unmetered favor that would get him the tip all this good time Charlie stuff was aimed at.

"We can walk back from there, if need be."

The driver let it go. At the highway, he waited for the light to change. You could see a mile in either direction and there was no traffic, not at this hour, but the driver was not going to cross against a red light and why should he? Crowe began to hate the sonofabitch who had timed the intervals of the light. Maybe during the day it made sense, but this was unbelievable.

"Maybe it's broke," Madeline said, addressing Crowe.

Across the road a big, lighted sign flashed AIRPORT MOTEL. Neon tubing edged the building. It was no Holiday Inn. The light changed, and the cab crossed the highway. It creaked to a stop at the office.

"I'll go in and see," Madeline said, pushing the door open.

The driver laughed. "They're not full."

"Give me some money."

The flickering sign advertized rooms at $19.95. Crowe sat forward to get his wallet out of his back pocket. He gave her a twenty. The door slammed and Madeline scooted under the little canopy and went inside. He handed a five to the driver.

"Hey, that's all right. This was a favor." But he had a good grip on the five.

"Thanks."

He pushed the door open, got out and slammed it. When he turned Madeline came out the office door, smiling like a kid, flourishing a key. She stooped to wave at the taxi driver, then once more was tugging Crowe into the unknown.

At unit 7, she handed him the key and took shelter under the dripping eave while he unlocked the door. Before he could reach in and turn on the lights, she had slipped inside. He found the lights before he closed the door, trying not to notice that the room was cold and smelled of old tobacco smoke and newer disinfectant. Madeline, head tipped back, was looking at a thermostat.

"There's no way to turn this thing up."

Crowe closed the drapes and flipped up the little lid of the combination air conditioner and heater. He punched Heat and then Fan. A promising roar filled the room.

"Sounds like we're about to take off." But she said it like a kid, excited; there was nothing else in her voice. He could still feel her hot little hand clutching his. She slipped out of her backpack and dropped it with a clunk in the corner and turned to him.

"You want to go first?"

"Go ahead."

"I went back there at the airport." She made it sound miles away.

"I can wait." He picked up the remote control and turned on the television.

"Okay if I take a shower?"

He nodded, not turning, as if it were the most ordinary question in the world. She had closed the bathroom door behind her before the porn movie flashed onto the screen, at least six people going at it in every way you could imagine while a little dog circled the scene yapping expectantly. Crowe plunged the screen into darkness. From behind the closed door of the bathroom the sound of a shower began.

It was another moment when he might have left. The thing

27

to do was to get the hell out of this town and head for a far part of the country and just stay out of sight for a while. All he had done was hit that kid, Larry, and the girl was the only witness and she obviously didn't give a damn. She would move on to somebody else without looking back. So what? But the fat lady and her stand-up comic of a husband had seen him with the girl. So had the taxi driver. The room clerk? Crowe realized he didn't know how Madeline had signed them in, but in a hot sheet place like this it wouldn't matter. Maybe. There were too many maybes. He imagined telling Lorenzo about this job, and he knew what the verdict would be.

There were cars for the taking in the motel parking lot; he could be abandoning the vehicle in Chicago in a couple hours, get some sleep and then pull out of there for a couple months. Somewhere hot and sunny where he could get drunk without worrying about who might recognize him.

He hung his topcoat in the closet, took off his jacket and lay down on the bed with his hands behind his head, listening to the sound of the shower. She was determined to get her money's worth, or his. The thought of money reminded him why he had come. Protecting himself had been uppermost in his mind since things started to unravel in the parking lot, but not doing what he had come to do would cost him fifty thousand dollars. Fifty thousand dollars and another name on the list of those he thought of as his retirement policy. Sharing that kind of secret with people would continue to be lucrative into the distant future.

He reviewed the events of the last hour again, trying to see them as harmless. And he succeeded, except for the body of that kid lying over there in the long-term parking lot of the airport. It could lie there till morning, maybe, but when the body was discovered the alarm would go off. But the more Crowe thought about it, the clearer it was that the only one who could link him with the body was Madeline.

The shower stopped, but the thin sound of her singing went on. When she came out, she was wrapped in a towel which she tugged about her as she looked around the room.

"Your turn," she said.

He swung his legs off the bed and tried to look casual as he went toward the bathroom, as if this was something he did every day of the week. Not many women understood how doing without it for so long affected you.

"Hey."

He turned.

"This is the only shower towel."

She unwrapped herself and the towel came flying across the room to him. He grabbed it and stepped into the bathroom, pulling the door shut behind him, but the fleeting glimpse of her body had both excited and repelled him. He turned on the shower, as much for her benefit as his own, wondering what lay ahead. He undressed, consulting his face in the mirror from time to time, hoping he might have some advice for himself. The showerhead wouldn't budge so he got a hot steady jet of water in the lower chest. He thought of singing too, but couldn't start. He gave up trying to ignore what lay ahead.

Whatever happened was her idea, not his. She had picked him up, after all, and it was her idea to come to this motel. When she threw the towel at him, giving him a glimpse of the promised land, she had removed any remaining doubt. He felt a sudden anger at her. Only whores acted like that, and she wasn't a whore. She'd starve as a whore, he assured himself, and couldn't help grinning. But the grin disappeared when he realized that he could hardly wait to get out there to her.

He turned off the water and stepped from the shower. The

towel was not too wet, but then how much water could a thin little body like hers accumulate? Standing naked in the steamy room, he draped the towel around his lower body. His legs were thin but his torso was full, muscular, with not too much hair. He turned out the light before opening the door.

The room was dark and quiet, but light bled through the drape from the large sign outside, flickering, pulsing. He moved slowly to the bed, and then it was firm against his shin. The covers had been pulled back. He let the towel drop to the floor and slipped under the covers. He lay as he had earlier, on his back, hands behind his head.

"Madeline," he said softly. Perhaps too softly. There was no reply. He reached out his hand to touch her. There was no head on the pillow beside his own.

He leapt from the bed and turned on the light. She was gone. Anger battled with a feeling of ridiculousness as he pulled on his clothes. The closet was open. His topcoat and jacket lay on the floor. There had been nothing in either of them. He did not like to think what would have happened if he had undressed before going into the bathroom. Had she expected the thrown towel to bring him to her?

He knelt and felt beneath the bed. He widened the arc of his hand. Then, his cheek pressed flat against the filthy carpet, he added sight to feeling.

She had taken his gun.

Four

Madeline stuffed the gun into her backpack as she ran toward the road. The overhead semaphore was still controlling imaginary traffic. Across the road, the airport looked like Christmas, rows of lights tracing runways, blinking lights on the tower, the lamps burning in the parking lots. Her heart was still in her mouth, but she wanted to shout with triumph. She could hardly wait to turn the gun over to Larry.

"Trust me," he had said when she knelt behind him in the parking lot, cradling his head, feeling for blood, but there wasn't any. "I moved with it."

She didn't smile. He had to feel he was in total control, no surprises. He was going to be the best there was. "I'm an apprentice," he said when she asked what he did. And he wouldn't tell her more. "The less you know the safer you are."

"Safe from who?"

"Me."

She loved his smile, but even more she loved his eyes. He was still working on his eyes. You should never smile with your eyes. He had dozens of rules like that. Madeline pretended he was learning to be an actor, but even so he took some getting used to. He was the best looking guy she had ever had.

In the parking lot, he showed her how to open a car, or at least he tried to. Finally he did it himself, and she got him settled in the back seat of a parked car. It was so dry and snug, he let her take him in his arms. She held him tight as she watched the man who had hit Larry finally leave the lot. She told Larry.

"He's just leaving?"

"Uh huh."

"I thought I was out for hours."

The car started down the road toward the highway, and Madeline was annoyed at how slow the guy was driving. And then he turned off. My God, he was coming back.

Larry sat up and watched too.

"You sure that's the guy?"

"Yes."

"What the hell."

She could feel Larry tighten up when the car turned in at short-term parking. Even from that distance, because of the light over the area, she saw the arm come out as he punched the button to get the ticket that would raise the barrier. They both sat forward now, arms on the back of the driver's seat, holding their breath as they watched the car.

"He's coming back to see how bad I am," Larry decided.

"Why would he do that?" Madeline didn't doubt him. It was a crazy explanation, but it was an explanation. Only it was the wrong one.

"He's going into the terminal."

"To fly back to Chicago."

"There are no more flights tonight." It had been her job to check that out.

"Then he should know that," Larry said, sounding more scared than puzzled.

"There are no buses either." It had made it easier that the terminal was for buses, trains and planes. "Why didn't he just keep the car he had?"

"Because he thinks you saw him in it."

32

"He sounds like you."

Larry made a little snorting sound. "Yeah."

"Look up there," she said excitedly, when the man's face appeared in the window over the entrance. "That's him."

"Are you sure?"

"Yes." She didn't know how she was sure, but she was. Every time she had seen him was from a distance, but she was certain he was the man in the window. Suddenly Larry was back in form.

"Get out and wave at him."

"I will not."

"Do what I tell you. This is going to turn out better than I thought."

She didn't wave, she just stood there, under the lamp in the parking lot, looking toward the window. When he shaded his eyes and leaned close to the glass she knew he had seen her. She held her stance and then he was gone. She practically fell back into the car.

"He saw you," Larry said.

"Let's get out of here."

"Not yet."

Out of nothing, it seemed, he had come up with this great idea. She would go in there, find the guy and make a move on him.

"I will not."

"Mad, we're on a job," he said sternly.

The plan was that she would hook up with him, Larry would be close by, she would keep in touch and soon they'd join up. It made no sense and she said so.

"I trust you, Mad. We have to trust one another."

That spooky hour with Crowe had been meant to prove to Larry that he could trust her. Madeline couldn't believe how well she had done. Taking Crowe's gun had been an inspira-

tion that came because ringing in her head all along was
Larry's warning. "Remember, he's armed."

A horn tooted out of the darkness before she reached the
highway. Madeline felt exposed and alone. The road leading
into the airport and its parking lots looked miles long. Another toot.

God. She couldn't go back to the motel, and the farther
she got from it the more vulnerable she was. And then she
heard Larry's piercing whistle, the one he said only dogs were
meant to hear.

"Thanks a lot."

He had grabbed her and held her close when she said that.
He liked her jokes. Not many people did, not any other guy
she'd known. Larry was more serious than any of them, but
he had a sense of humor. His whistle in those circumstances
had the effect of a joke, altering her mood immediately,
making her want to laugh out loud. He was waiting in the
brightly lit lot of a rental car company's used car division.

She wanted to run right into his arms, but he demanded a
report first. They got into a car, and she handed him the gun.

"He never touched me."

"Good."

Did he care? He was holding the gun so it caught the light
better.

"I wonder what he's done with this baby?"

"Where to now?"

"Let's see what he does."

Back with Larry, she had forgotten the fear she had felt
when she was with Crowe. The shower was the only way she
could think of to get away from him, and what if he had suggested they shower together? It was that kind of a motel and
he had every right to think she was ready for anything. That
had been her assignment, after all. That's why Larry hadn't

reacted when she told him Crowe hadn't touched her. Maybe he didn't even believe her.

"The point is, it doesn't matter."

"It does to me."

"Because you love me?"

"Yes."

"Baby, this is just another way of showing it. You think it would matter if I had to bang some doll to insure a job went off right? You think that would do anything to us?"

"I wouldn't ask you to do that."

What a hoot. Men took it wherever and whenever, and Larry was a man. He was right about men not getting attached to someone just because they'd been to bed together; most men couldn't wait to get out of bed once it was over. The only thing that held them was the chance of doing it again.

"Taking the gun, that was good."

He kissed her then, a thank you kiss, but with the promise of more. She shivered at the thought that she might have spent the night in that motel bed with the man they had been following about for nearly two weeks.

At that moment Crowe burst out of the motel, pulling on his topcoat and looking from right to left as he ran. Before he reached the road, he stopped. He looked toward the motel, then turned back again, walking toward a parked car. Larry's arm tightened around her as he watched. Within minutes the man had the car running and was backing away from the motel. Larry started the motor of the car they were in.

"You've got a key."

"I stopped by the office first, since I had time."

At the highway, Crowe hesitated, as if he were waiting for that light to change, then turned right, toward the town. Larry fell in behind him, keeping a discreet distance in the all but deserted streets.

Five

At ten o'clock, Lucy checked the answering machine again, but Crowe hadn't left the message. He was the most cautious man she had ever known, not that she knew him; they hadn't even met. She suspected that, if it were possible, he would have insisted that the arrangements be made without their ever meeting. It had taken a long time to discover that he was indeed the man she was looking for. She even went back to Lorenzo to ask if he hadn't made a mistake. His answering smile included three gold-capped teeth.

"That's Crowe," he said approvingly. "Now you wouldn't expect a man in his line of work to just start doing business with a stranger."

"I've done everything you said."

"Be patient."

Patient. She hated the word, but it was the word that connected her with both Dr. Lodge and with the elusive Crowe.

"And don't mention my name."

"No."

"I mean that. You haven't told him of your old friend Lorenzo here at Michigan City?" He leaned toward her, as if he would know if she were lying. The truth was she hadn't thought that mentioning Lorenzo would have any appreciable effect on Crowe.

One did not look up hired assassins in the Yellow Pages, of course. She would not have wanted anyone less elusive than

Crowe; still it was annoying that it took so long as they inched toward speaking right out about why she had called him. But it did help that Lorenzo was not surprised.

"Who you want hit?"

"Lorenzo. You don't expect me to tell you that."

"Protecting yourself?"

"Isn't that Rule One?"

"You already broke it, honey, talking to me."

"Who'd believe you?" She laughed.

"You got something there."

Of course she did. She had already, in remarks she made to the assistant warden, planted a covering story. Lorenzo thought his life would make a good book, and she had encouraged him to talk about it.

"It's not half as interesting as he thinks, of course."

The assistant warden, a young woman with acne and enormous breasts looked as if she liked being locked up with all those desperate men. What draws people into correctional work? The same thing that had made her a volunteer at the prison, she supposed. Morbid curiosity. There was something awe inducing about rows of cells containing men who had ruined the only life they had.

"He's my proto-jay," Lorenzo said. He was enlarging his vocabulary and had to use a new word at least three times. "Ain't that rich? Crowe's my jay."

Lorenzo had a narrative gift, there was no doubt about it. It was possible that if he talked naturally with a tape recorder going, a powerful book could be made of it. He was the oddest combination of brilliance and stupidity.

"Can't you just get word to him, Lorenzo?"

He shook his head emphatically. "One, he don't trust me. Two, he won't trust you. Three, he trusts nobody."

"Is there anyone else?"

"There is no one else like Crowe. He is as good as I was."
He paused. "I know what you're thinking. If he stays out of
here, he's better than I was."

So it became a little research project. Where was Philip
Crowe? And, if she found him, how would she be able to talk
to him about what Lorenzo assured her Crowe did for a
living? She had to ask him with reasonable directness how
much he charged to kill someone.

While he was on parole from Michigan City, on a charge of
auto theft, Crowe had become a model of what the prison
system should regularly do, return a man to society as a pro-
ductive citizen. He lectured to high school groups, he helped
parole officers with recalcitrant wards, he said fervently that
he never intended to spend another day in prison. But when
his parole ended, he dropped from sight.

"I mean from our sight," Ewell the probation officer said,
moving his lips which in turn moved his mustache, as if he
were trying to get his mouth to rotate. "In this job, you see the
seamy side and not much else. What's your interest in
Crowe?"

"My interest? I'm doing this for a prisoner I help at Michigan City."

"Anyone I know?"

"Lorenzo White."

Ewell's mustache settled down and was still. "What's he
want with Crowe?"

"I think he used to know him."

"Do you know what Lorenzo is in for? He was a paid assassin. God knows how many people he killed." He stopped
and looked at her. "He could be setting Crowe up."

"They were friends."

"People in prison are strange." He looked away, then decided not to go on about that. She thought she knew what he

meant. It seemed unfair to Lorenzo, serving a life sentence, to be heaping on his head crimes of which he was innocent. Talking about Crowe was just a way for Lorenzo to talk about himself.

"You ought to look him up," Lorenzo had suggested.

"You're more than I can handle."

"You're right about that, honey."

She had not objected to his way of talking to her; maybe she had found it flattering. The danger of becoming a prison groupie no longer seemed remote. But her visit to Dr. Lodge had put everything into a different light.

If Crowe had dropped out of sight when his parole was over, he had kept in touch with Lorenzo. Not that he had visited the prison at Michigan City. When he vowed that he would never go back there he meant as visitor as well as inmate. He was dedicating the rest of his life to becoming a totally different man from the one who had been sent to prison.

"You said he visits you."

"He calls me on the telephone."

"The phones are monitored."

"He calls me as Benjie Lautreamont."

Kid stuff. Fool teacher. But when the time came when she wanted to hire the sort of killer Lorenzo had been, Lucy was tolerant of all the subterfuges and secrecy with which Philip Crowe conducted himself.

Blinking, Lucy glanced at the probation officer. "Do you think he'll ever be sent back?" she asked Ewell.

"He served out his parole."

"I mean on something else."

Ewell didn't think so. "I never met a man who hated prison so much."

"But does he hate crime?"

"Is that one of Lorenzo's questions?"

She was employing the ruse of putting to him questions for Lorenzo's imaginary book. "Mine."

"He might."

"But then I might. Or you might."

Warren, as he had seemed to her before Dr. Lodge's revelation, was simply absorbed in his work and lived by the charming assumption that anything he did was more interesting than anything she did or could possibly do. He had shown little interest in any of her doings, except insofar as he thought of them as indirectly advancing his own career, and her visits to the state prison were no exception.

"Make sure you get out before they lock up," he said, surprising himself with what he took to be the wit of the remark. He used it whenever the subject came up, including their regular dinner with the Kramers a week after she got the news. "You should get on the prison detail too," he said to Yolande.

"Oh I wouldn't be very good at that."

This charity of Lucy's fascinated Max. "What exactly do you do there?"

"Help the prisoners who need it with their letters. I only do it once a month. It doesn't loom large in my life." At the moment nothing loomed so large in her life as the leaving of it.

"It's okay with me," Warren said. "Just as long as she leaves before they lock up."

The Kramers laughed almost as heartily as Warren. It was, Lucy realized, one of the few things approaching a witticism he had ever uttered. Had she ever really loved him?

Warren as he seemed to her after Lodge's revelation was not a lovable man. But in this he did not differ from others, including herself. She told herself that it was unfair to judge people and things in her present state; it was like tasting things when she had a fever—sweet things tasted flat, sour things bland. They really tasted that way when one had a fever, but that is not what they were really like. The world looked at by one under sentence of death could not be what it was really like.

But the analogy did not hold. Having a fever was an aberration, a condition that came and went, when one was restored to normal. But it had always been true that she was going to die. That it should be by cancer was a variable, but that it must and would happen was simply the way things are. Not being aware of it was the sickness, the coated tongue that kept reality at bay. Warren was deceitful and untrue. But he was especially repellant to her now because like everyone else, like herself before the visit to Lodge, he was going through life in a fit of distraction, refusing to face up to the fact that he must die.

In a dream she had shortly afterward, a crowd of people moved through a scented field where flowers bloomed, birds swooped overhead, and fleecy clouds created a Disney effect. But the field ended in a sheer drop which was concealed by the sweet knee-high grass. People plunged pell mell through the grass and suddenly dropped soundlessly from sight, yet the others were so enthralled by the beauty of the field that they did not notice until they too dropped out of sight. Lucy who could see it all as clear as clear tried to shout in warning, but no sound issued from her throat.

She awoke to the realization that she was fortunate to have learned the truth from Lodge. He had made it sound like an incredible intrusion into the normal state of things, and that is how she had reacted. But surely a doctor must know that death is inevitable for everyone. Pretending it isn't so seemed to be a condition for living at all.

Lucy's advantage was that she need not wait for it to

happen. She would go freely forward to meet her fate.

But tastefully. She did not want to open her veins in the bath in the manner of ancient pagans and Hollywood actresses. That called attention to oneself and carried with it the false suggestion that for such a one to die was news. If she had known more, she would have known undetectable ways of taking her life. But even if she had known, there was Dr. Lodge to take into account. He of course would suspect something; as a friend of Warren's he might say something. The one thing she was adamant about was that she wanted no one to be pained by her death. Above all she did not want to excite remorse and sorrow in Warren. He wasn't much of a husband, but then she hadn't been much of a wife. In this they seemed pretty much like everybody else, so it was silly to make a point of it.

Arranging her own death was to be a matter between Lucy and herself. Lorenzo's friend Philip Crowe would be her instrument. All he would ask was money. How sad that was. She imagined him standing over the corpses of the human race, possessed of all the stones and metals considered precious, all the currencies of the world, awaiting the inevitable hit man within.

Arranging her own death led on to thoughts of tidying up other matters as well. She realized that she was not as indifferent to Warren's affair with Yolande as she had thought.

"Who is the subject?" Crowe asked when she finally phoned him.

"A woman."

A pause. "She married?"

He assumed it was a rival, her husband's mistress, perhaps. How much did he need to know?

"Do you care?"

"I have to know all the complications."

"I will provide photographs, habits, a day and an hour."

"Sounds like you don't need me."

"Oh yes I do."

"Is it you?"

That was when she knew she had the right man. "Would it matter?"

"There are crazy doctors who'd do it for nothing."

"I want a professional."

One brief bark of a laugh on the line. "When?"

"It's not me," she had lied.

"I didn't think so."

"I want it done soon."

"No. I don't work that way. There are precautions."

And he went through them, beginning of course with the money. After all, this was a business arrangement. He did not want money that would link him with the death. Then there was method.

"I don't suppose you want violence."

"That doesn't matter. Speed would be nice."

It was the strangest conversation she had ever had. She had phoned him from her car at a number that was clearly a public phone, outside. It sounded like mall traffic behind him as they spoke of how he would bring about her death. She said that, yes, she knew about stun guns from her work with SPCA. On television she had watched wild animals rendered helpless in seconds and without pain by a projectile that injected them with a powerful sedative. The point was it could be more than a sedative.

"That's pretty sensational, isn't it?"

"You mean it raises the question of who did it?"

That isn't what she had meant, but there was that as well.

In the end she had left the method to him. It would be swift and sure, that was all she really cared about, that and the avoidance of the sensational. The arrangement was that he would leave a message on her answering machine—the innocuous message that her alterations were ready—and she would know she had three days. If she wished to change arrangements—call it off, postpone it, set a definite time and place—she still had time.

But there was still no message on the answering machine. She rewound it and listened to every message that hadn't been erased. Warren looked out of his den.

"I thought someone was talking out here."

"I'm checking messages."

"Again?"

So he had heard her earlier.

Six

"I hate the way she condescends to you," Yolande had said to Warren a year ago, when it began. She had left Lucy in the Ladies room and come back to the table while Max was talking to the manager about the wine they had been served.

"Does she?"

"You know she does."

"I'm too busy trying to peek down your dress." He moved his hand toward her daring décolletage and she backed away, reluctantly, Warren thought. He liked that in a woman. Not in his wife, however; that is why he had married Lucy. She was to be the perfect mother of the children they never had.

"You're awful."

"I thought it was Lucy who was awful."

"Don't you care?"

"Not if you do."

She looked at him with the little smile she must have learned in Psychology 101. "Why do you stand it? You're not Catholic. Life doesn't have to be like that, you know. People can be happy."

"It's in the bill of rights."

"Not having it, the pursuit of it."

"I'm all for pursuit. When can I see you?"

Psychology 101 again. "Is that your idea of a solution?"

"What's yours?"

"We have very different problems."

45

Max was attentive, dutiful in performing his tasks as a husband, by which of course she meant in the bedroom. She whispered the rest in his ear, hot breath coiling, then entering the inner ear, throwing him off balance. "But he's dull."

In the circumstances, the suggestion was that Warren was good at it, interesting, diverting. Her husband wasn't. By which she meant, though probably did not know it, that Warren did whatever she asked him to do. She was surprisingly agile and seemingly insatiable. It was exciting, but not what he wanted in his wife. As he wouldn't tell Yolande, he liked Lucy just the way she was. He loved her in the fundamental sense that he had linked his life with hers and meant to keep his promise. Yolande was a diversion. And of course one that must be kept a secret from Lucy.

So he felt sneaky about Yolande, as he had about the others. Not that there were all that many. But the others had been anonymous, women met at conventions in other towns, hotel women, left behind as you checked out of the room. Yolande was the first among their friends. When he feared being found out the excuse that leapt to his lips was that Yolande made him do it. And she had.

It began at the club, when he had taken advantage of an afternoon only to find that kids had commandeered the pool.

"Is Lucy here?"

Yolande plopped into the chair beside him and as they talked her arms lifted as she did something to her hair, an operation that had the effect of presenting her breasts to him. All he would have had to do is move his head a few inches and he could snap at them.

Her excuse probably would have been that he acted from the outset as if something were going to happen. With Yolande he had surprised in himself a gift for facetious comment, the sort of talk he avoided around Lucy.

"I never see her in the pool."

"There's a reason for that."

"What?"

"She doesn't swim."

"Doesn't swim." Her hands descended along the firm lines of her sides. Warren had never seen her twice in the same suit.

"She knows how to. She just doesn't enjoy it." He looked around. "This isn't a typical day."

"Does she golf?"

He shrugged. There were men who professed to enjoy golfing with their wives. He was not one of them. Actually, Lucy was a natural golfer, as he himself was not. His game was the product of many expensive lessons and a penchant to buy the latest in gimmicky clubs.

"She hasn't time."

"She doesn't work, does she?"

"Not in that sense, no. But she's very busy."

"Oh, I know." Yolande said this as if she had hit upon Lucy's basic flaw. Lucy was busy because it was a way of not facing up to her unsatisfactory marriage. That was pretty strong, but Warren was fascinated with the way the movement of her breasts accompanied what she said.

"Do you know the French word for brassiere?"

"Isn't it already a French word?" But a little wondering smile formed on her plush lips.

"Soutien-gorge."

"What does it mean?"

"I was hoping you knew."

She laughed, her breasts laughed, all of her laughed. Later she would explain that his verbal horniness was an attempt to compensate for a loveless marriage. He should have been repelled by this simplistic understanding of human beings and of her presumptuous remarks about his marriage, but it was the price he had to pay for her consolations.

"Does anyone ever get enough?" he asked.

He had her. If she said no, he had her, if she said yes, he had her, because the point of all this solicitude would disappear. Warren already suspected that in describing his imaginary frustration she was really describing her own. She said nothing.

"How often do you suppose people do it?" he asked.

"Married people?"

"Yes."

"I'd be more interested in what you think."

"Thinking has nothing to do with it."

With her he felt like a stand-up comic; she laughed at everything he said. He realized she was nervous. It was risky to come sit next to him like that, wearing only a stunning bathing suit, gossip being what it was around the club.

"I'm going in."

"You'll get wet."

He watched her swim, but in that he did not differ from most of the others around the pool. Yolande had a magnificent body and pool time was her chance to expose herself with impunity. Every move she made was meant to be watched, but if you enjoyed watching you were some kind of pervert.

And so it began, as the novels Yolande read probably put it. Her place, when Max was away and the kids at camp, once or twice at a motel. She liked it in the tub, on the floor, the bed was for the last one. Warren felt like a sexual athlete. Yolande of course had read books and watched the raunchier kind of programs on cable aimed at helping viewers come to terms with their sexuality. Her theory of sex made it miraculous that the race had found a way to continue itself throughout all those millennia without enlightened views of sex.

"But that's just it. They thought it was only for reproduction."

"Thank God. What if Adam used condoms."

Lucy did not suspect because she thought too highly of him to imagine he would carry on an affair, let alone be stupid enough to do it right under her nose, let alone, further, that he would waste time with a centerfold like Yolande. Or was it Yolande's centerfold? The two couples began to have dinner together once a week. Dropping Yolande proved to be more difficult than getting started with her.

"Does Lucy know?"

"Does Max?"

"Max," she repeated, making a face. By now he knew all about Max, or at least what Yolande wanted him to think about Max. "I think he's bisexual."

"Maybe he has bivalves."

"Of course it's just a suspicion."

"He is impeccable in the locker room."

Somewhere, Yolande was sure, there were places where happy people frolicked, taking one another at will, and without consequences, regrets or the usual hangups. She had read of places in California.

It was at dinner with the Kramers that Warren noticed a change in Lucy. Her manner was different in some undefinable way. At one point, while Yolande was talking, Warren saw Lucy looking at her with an expression he had never before seen. His first panicky thought was that she knew about himself and Yolande.

"Have a good time?" he asked her later.

She looked at him as if she hadn't understood the question.

"At the club."

She nodded slightly. "Never better."

"Oh, it wasn't as nice as all that."

"We're just making talk, aren't we?"

"It's what people do."

"I know."

This was bad. Something was very different than before, far more than he had thought at dinner. "You feeling all right?"

"Of course."

"I wonder if you aren't overdoing it, Lucy. You work harder than people who work."

"Maybe you're right."

"We should plan a trip, get away from it all, you know."

"That's a good idea."

"I'll have Marion get to work on it." Marion, his secretary, thrived on making travel arrangements, probably because she seldom went anywhere herself.

"No. I'll do it."

"Good."

Then why didn't he feel good?

For several days the feeling that something indefinable was wrong persisted. He became preoccupied. He did odd things, things he hoped would absorb him pointlessly, keep his mind off his growing uneasiness. That was why he actually sat down with their car phone bills and studied them. Most of the numbers she called he knew. For no reason, he decided to dial the one he didn't recognize.

The first time he tried he got a busy signal. He tried again five minutes later with the same result. It became a matter of principle to reach that number. But throughout the day, whenever he dialed, the number was busy. He felt almost frantic now, which was crazy, but then it was crazy to call the number in the first place. And then, ready to slam down the phone when the busy signal began, he heard a ring.

He pressed the phone to his ear, excited. It rang and rang and rang without answer. How could a phone that was always busy not be answered?

"Yeah," a voice said.

"Hello, who's this?"

"Who do you want?"

"Have I got the right number?"

"You have if you're calling a public phone."

"A public phone! Where?"

But the line went dead. He called back and once more got the busy signal. Why would Lucy call a pay phone?

Warren's imagination ran wild as he recalled Lucy's recent strangely preoccupied behavior. What was she hiding? What was she doing that was so incriminating she had to make contact with someone at a pay phone?

Seven

Crowe drove halfway back to Chicago, stopping at Michigan City. The first thing he did was go to the Yokohama Spa where he got a massage from an anonymous smiling Oriental of indeterminate origin. She didn't look Japanese to him. The motel he went to was like the one across the road from the Michiana Airport. He let himself in, locked the door, and lay fully dressed on the bed.

"Like everything else, you think you're good and you're dead," Lorenzo had once told him. "Look at me here. Why?" Because he had made the most elementary mistake that can be made when you're following someone. Not looking out for someone following *you*. "On that occasion, there seemed no reason to be careful in making connections. Maybe if I had thought about it I would have said no, that's crazy, ain't no one even know who you is or that you is in town, let alone want to follow you." Lorenzo had dipped his eye, showing a lot of white as he stared at Crowe. "I was wrong."

It had been the mistake that got him put away. Lorenzo was being followed by a cop who put him together with something else, years before, and just got curious. Crowe wondered now if Madeline was connected with someone he'd taken a job on? But someone bent on revenge would already have taken it. She had found the gun that would have made that easy.

Crowe could not forget the gun. To remember it was to realize it was his ticket back to the row alongside Lorenzo. Was that what she meant to do, turn in the weapon that would be linked to at least six unsolved killings?

After lying there a while in the dark motel room he could see as well as if he had the light on. One thing was clear. He had to get that gun, and when he had it he would use it on the girl. Getting fifty miles between him and that airport motel still seemed the smart thing to do, but what the next move should be he didn't know. If he hadn't lost the gun he was certain he would retire right now, take what he had and just go somewhere and get lost. He had ID of various kinds that would enable him to set up in different ways. He had money, more than enough. But without the gun he would spend the rest of his life wondering when it would hook him up again with the past.

But it was rage more than caution that made him determined to get that gun. The only thing he knew about that girl was her name and she probably made that up. How had she registered?

He sat up. She had run through the rain to the office and gotten the room. It was the only lead he had and by God he meant to follow it. He fell asleep but even in his sleep he continued to think about the predicament he had gotten himself into. What he kept hearing was the voice of that kid in the parking lot.

"Something wrong?"

It might have been an omen.

He switched cars before heading back the next morning. Memories of Lorenzo's downfall came to him and he made frequent checks in the rearview mirror, convinced it was pointless. But maybe it wasn't. If he had been a betting man he would have put something on the chance that the little red Mustang was on his tail. He pulled into an oasis to check it out. The Mustang followed him in.

He slung his bag over his shoulder and went inside and into the john, exiting it immediately and going into the game room to the left of the entrance. There were two people in the Mustang, the driver and someone in the passenger seat. Crowe waited. Five minutes, ten minutes. Finally the driver's door swung open. The guy who got out looked like the twin of the kid he had decked in the airport parking lot the night before. He went to the car Crowe had been driving, checking it out, then sauntered back to the Mustang. Mr. Casual. So he had survived. Crowe was sure it was the Good Samaritan from the South Bend airport parking lot. And he was pretty damned sure who was in the passenger seat of the Mustang. And then the kid was coming toward the oasis.

Crowe was concealed by Space Invaders when the kid went by. Immediately, Crowe ran outside to the Mustang, pulled open the door and slipped behind the wheel. The girl cried out, but he brought his arm back and she shriveled into the seat. He turned the key, started the motor and took off.

"Where you been?" she asked, when they were moving.

"In the shower."

"You smell nice."

"Thanks. Where is it?"

"It?"

"What you took from beneath the bed."

"In my knapsack. Should I get it out?"

"You move at all, and I'll shove you right out that door."

"I'm wearing my seat belt."

She was a brazen little bitch, he gave her that. He still hadn't looked at her, not wanting to be reminded of what a goddam fool he'd made of himself before. Now he had a chance to get the edge back, and he didn't mean to lose it.

"Who's your friend?"

"Aren't you my friend?"

He pressed the release on her seat belt, gunning the motor as he did. "It's more effective at high speed," he explained.

She gripped the handle over the door. "You mean Larry?"

"I guess I didn't hit him hard enough."

"He said he moved with the blow."

Crowe was keeping an eye on the mirror, but so far there was only the traffic he had moved into.

"Talk," he said.

"About what?"

The panel to his left enabled him to unlock the passenger door and she moved away from it, making a grab for his arm, but he pushed her away. She began to struggle with the seat belt, then got it hooked again.

"Start with why you're following me."

"I don't know."

His hand moved to release the seat belt.

"I don't know," she screamed. "He never told me."

He rolled into roadside parking and found a place away from the truckers. When the car was parked he turned to her.

"Listen, and listen good. For what you did last night, you're dead. Understand that. You are under sentence of death." He was looking at her for the first time, and he saw the terror in her eyes. "The only question is when and how." He paused to make sure she understood. "Now, talk. Tell me about Larry, tell me why you just happened to look under that bed and take my weapon."

Not taking his eyes from her, he reached over the seat and got her backpack. He flipped it open and dug around in it, not really believing the gun would be there, but it was. He took it out, glanced at it, and put it back in the holster. He felt like a steer who has been restored to status and now rules the field. She had watched his movements with wide frightened eyes.

She was relieved when he put the gun away.

"Larry has an uncle named Lorenzo. He's named after him."

Lorenzo!

"Go on."

"He wants to be like him. Lorenzo told him of you."

"Told him what?"

"You know."

"Tell me."

"That you kill people."

"Lorenzo wouldn't tell him that."

She brightened. "You know Lorenzo, don't you?"

"I know lots of Lorenzos. It's a common name."

She tried to laugh. Her hair was dry and shiny and he wondered if she had slept with Larry last night. They would have followed him to Michigan City, probably stayed in the same motel. No probably about it. He knew it before she said yes, of course.

"Why?"

"He says he's your apprentice. Yours and Lorenzo's. He wanted to do your job for you."

"What job?"

"That's the problem. He doesn't know."

"And he thought I'd tell him?"

"We came down here on the train with you. After we got here, Larry thought he could join up with you. That's why he followed you into the parking lot to help you get a car. He thought you would be grateful, ask him along . . ."

"Larry sounds like a stupid sonofabitch."

"You're his hero."

"He doesn't know me."

"He knows what Lorenzo told him."

Was it possible that Lorenzo had told some kid about him?

Crowe thought about it. Everyone was capable of stupidity. Think of last night. Think of how Lorenzo had ended up, just because he hadn't followed the rules. The follower can always be followed. In a way he owed it to Lorenzo that he had noticed the red Mustang in his mirror.

"Where'd he pick up this car?"

"In South Bend."

"Where abouts?"

"The used car lot of the rental agency."

"He get the key in the office?"

"Yes."

That meant Crowe couldn't risk driving the Mustang back into town. It would have been reported by now. In fact, it was stupid to be sitting in it. That was when he saw the Lincoln roll in. A Lincoln. The kid must be crazy.

"Here's Larry," he said.

"Yeah."

"Wave him down."

"You going to hurt him?"

The way she said it made it clear that she had been acting last night. Or playing whore to Larry's pimp.

"Not if you do what you're told."

"Is it okay if I open the door?"

"Open it."

He hit the horn when the Lincoln rolled by, and the girl jumped out and went waving to it. Crowe gave them time to talk a bit, then he got out of the Mustang and went to the Lincoln. He opened the back door and got in. Leather. Nice.

"I'm Larry."

"Hello, Larry."

"Where to?"

"The first exit."

And they were on their way. Crowe, his apprentice, and

57

the girl who had made a fool of them.

"Is that a phone?"

Madeline handed it to him, and he punched out the numbers. It rang and he waited for the answering machine to
come on, but she answered.

"Your alterations are ready."

"It's you."

"Call that number in an hour."

He hung up and handed the phone to Madeline.

Eight

"He's going to kill us," she whispered to Larry as the three of them walked through the mall.

Larry laughed. At last he was working with the famous Crowe, on his first job, really an apprentice now. He skipped ahead to walk beside Crowe, who ignored him of course. Madeline hated Larry acting like that. He was like a little kid, scampering along next to the big man and Crowe loved it, that was obvious. He no longer seemed the nervous unsure mark she had led on the night before. She was almost sorry she had ditched him like that.

But in the car, she had known he meant it when he said he'd kill her, and he hadn't taken it back either. The threat still stood, and it included Larry as much as her. He'd already tried to kill Larry once, and it was no fault of his if he hadn't. He would have left Larry lying there like so much garbage and not given it another thought and there was Larry licking the hand that beat him. He said he'd moved with the blow; that's why it hadn't done much more than knock him out. More likely it was his hard head.

All about them in the huge echoing mall, with music softening the noise, busy shoppers moved, their eyes bright with the prospect of buying. Places like this reminded Madeline that she was not like other people. Other people had parents and a house they grew up in, maybe brothers and sisters. Madeline had imagined a life like that for herself in the most

59

private part of her mind, and she would turn to it from time to time. She'd read somewhere that it was a common fantasy for kids to imagine that they had been adopted or kidnapped, that they weren't really their parents' child, but maybe a prince or princess. Madeline dreamed that she had been kidnapped from just an ordinary family. Her mother's name in this imagined version of herself was Maureen and her father was Joe. Just Joe. He worked of course and it didn't matter what he did; he brought home money and she and Maureen depended on him. Of course Maureen didn't work. There was the house and, in some versions of the fantasy, other children for her to worry about. But usually Madeline thought of herself as an only child, doted over and spoiled, but basically good. She and her mother would shop in malls like this one . . .

"Keep up," Larry said, frowning at her. He had dropped back and took her elbow to hurry her along.

"What's the rush?"

He made a disgusted sound, and she felt a sudden anger.

"Tell me if you know what's going on, because I don't. Killer, up there . . ."

His grip on her arm tightened painfully, and he leaned his face into hers. "Don't ever call him that again."

"Excuse me."

"I mean it, Mad."

Larry had pledged his loyalty to Crowe, whether or not the older man wanted it.

"Okay."

What did she expect? Last night he had let her do the tough stuff, even granted that he had just been whacked on the head with a gun. Whatever it took to form an attachment to Crowe was all right with Larry. She remembered her pathetic effort to tell him she and Crowe hadn't done anything.

Larry didn't care if they had or not. If she hadn't brought that gun out with her he would have sent her right back to Crowe's bed. If it came to that, he'd probably be willing to sleep with the guy himself. Not that she thought that was Crowe's problem. He was shy and inexperienced and of course he had all that violence weighing him down. What do you think of people after you've killed a few of them? Had he ever stayed around to see the result of his handiwork? Probably not. He would be disappearing into the woodwork as soon as the job was done.

They had come to a bank of pay phones. Crowe said to Larry, "That's the one."

A fat girl was using it, jabbering away affectedly while a short girl with a frizzy hairdo tried to follow the conversation. Larry went up, took the phone out of her hands and hung it up.

"This is an emergency," he explained.

The fat girl wasn't having any of that. She looked around, invoking universal amazement at what had just happened to her.

"You hung up that phone while I was in the midst of a very important conversation." Her voice trembled with indignation. She reached for the phone and Larry grabbed her wrist.

"Beat it."

The fat girl's expression changed as she began to feel the pain. No one seemed to care that this man had taken the phone away from her and hung it up.

"I'm going to report this."

"We're mall security," Larry said.

While this was going on, Madeline moved to Crowe's side.

"Crude but effective," he said. "He's doing everything but make a public announcement."

"He wants to impress you."

"Yeah."

"Don't hurt him."

His cold eyes rested on her briefly. She wanted to add, don't hurt me either. But she was certain he would do whatever he felt like doing. Larry was walking off with the fat girl and her little friend, pouring on the charm now. He was handing her a quarter, courtesy of the mall, to make her call at any other phone. The fat girl seemed mollified. Crowe looked on with something approaching approval.

Crowe took up the phone, keeping the hook depressed, appearing to be using it while he waited for it to ring.

"How long has it been?"

"I don't have a watch."

"Get one."

"Yes, sir."

He just looked at her. His face was so expressionless it was difficult to believe how he had looked in the motel when she threw him the shower towel. The phone rang, he released the hook, and turned away from her.

"Yeah."

He listened, saying almost nothing. Finally he nodded.

"You're the boss." And after a while, "If that's what you want, that's it."

Hope leapt in Madeline. The job was being called off. Except for taking a few cars, she and Larry had done nothing wrong. Larry had a chip on his shoulder and she understood that, but it made no sense to do what the people he hated expected him to do. Sometimes she thought that, subconsciously, Larry assumed it was his destiny to end up in jail. In the meantime, the thing to do was amass a record you could be proud of when you were locked up. Larry talked about prison as if it were a fraternity.

Larry came back just as Crowe was hanging up the phone. He turned.

"Not for two more days."

Larry nodded, as if this were old stuff. What a silly kid he was when you saw him next to a man. "You going back to Chicago?"

"No, but you two better."

"When do you want me back?"

"Why would I want you back?"

"Because you can't trust me."

"There are remedies for that."

"You can't trust Madeline either."

"She'd be first."

Larry laughed, as if Crowe was telling a joke. Maybe he was. The decision was that they would all remain in town. Crowe would stay in one motel, Larry in another.

"Who gets me?" Madeline asked.

She noticed that Larry waited for Crowe to decide.

Nine

When Lucy hung up her car phone she was stopped at an intersection. On either side of her, other cars waited for the light to change. She glanced at the man to her left who had the profile of a boxer. In the car on her right a girl moved her head to the jungle rhythms that blasted from her open windows. It was possible that either one of them might die before she did, of a heart attack, in a car accident, assaulted. They didn't know when the end would come, but she did. Knowing gave her a funny sense of power.

She had forty-eight hours to live.

The little lilt of fear she felt was to be expected. If death was natural, encoded in her nature, to fight against it was natural too. But the battle was foredoomed and she did not intend to wait patiently to be undone by the cancer eating away inside her. Her misgivings bore on the manner she had chosen to make her exit. Now, having given Crowe his final instructions, deciding in her role of governor not to grant a stay of execution, she had time to review the paths she had not taken.

Not for a moment had she been willing to undertake the course of surgery and chemotherapy that might have added some blighted months to her existence. Such a route required hope and Lodge had been unable to offer her hope, only postponement, and a painful and humiliating postponement at that. No thanks.

So suicide. One word for dozens of methods. She could hurl herself off a bridge into the St. Joseph River, she could go to the building where Warren had his office and take a last leap from a 12th story window. She could shoot, hang or poison herself. She could her quietus make with a bare bodkin.

She smiled. Where had that come from? She was driving past the Farmer's Market and continued along the river road, past the campus of Indiana University, and into Mishawaka. Further eastward were Mennonites and, to the south, Amish. The line was from Shakespeare, she was sure of that. Hamlet? Perhaps. Translated, it meant that one could stab oneself to death. Not in a million years. The thought of mutilating her body repelled her. What in the end she had decided on, with a relieved sense of its fittingness, was a method that would point the finger of blame at Warren.

If she were not under sentence of death, her vindictiveness would have appalled her. But she was now operating with a clarity of mind given only to those on the brink of the grave. Warren had been deceiving her for years. That, added to his condescension and generally odious personal traits, was too much. Lucy found herself quite unwilling to leave Warren free to pursue his affair with Yolande, perhaps break up her marriage with Max, or, more likely, widen the field of his activities and become that most ridiculous of figures, the aging Don Juan. The serious ambitions of his youth and the need for a marriage commensurate with those ambitions had kept Warren more or less in line, sexually speaking. More or less. The less had consisted largely of strange items on credit card bills that could be traced to his travels to other cities—silly, perhaps dangerous, such dalliance might be, but at least it had the merit of taking her feelings into account. His increasingly obvious affair with Yolande was different. And essential to her plans. The escorts and visiting masseuses with whom he frolicked in far off hotel rooms scarcely provided a motive, but Yolande emphatically did.

Lucy would so arrange her death that it would inevitably be interpreted as a husband's hiring an assassin to get rid of his wife to make room for his mistress. That was why the hired killer was important.

And why it was as Yolande Kramer that she had entered into dealings with the Philip Crowe she had heard of from Lorenzo, the object of her charitable concern at the state prison.

Her death would occur in two days and would be, she had been assured by Crowe, both swift and sure. Of course he thought it was Yolande expressing merciful concern for her victim, but no matter. Lucy dreaded the moment, but having no alternative now she meant that moment to serve further purposes. Warren and Yolande would both be implicated.

Max would be hurt by this, but he was a resilient man. He would find consolation in golf, in tennis, in jogging and in all the other activities by which he sought to keep age at bay.

She had spoken again with Dr. Lodge.

"Have you given further thought to our discussion of the other day?"

"I've thought of little else."

"Of course. May I ask if you intend to seek a second opinion?"

"Yes."

"Well . . ."

"I meant yes you may ask. The answer is no."

"You would be told exactly what I told you." He seemed relieved that she had accepted his verdict. "Have you decided about treatments?"

"Yes."

"Meaning yes?"

"Meaning no. I have accepted the inevitable."

A long pause. Should he go into detail on what she faced? "I wouldn't advise that. However discouraging treatment may seem, it can keep you going for some possible breakthrough . . ."

"I have accepted my fate."

Again, she was struck by how embarrassing he found the subject of death. Did he think it spelled failure of medical efforts? But surely he could not believe that there is or ever would be a cure for death.

"You would of course be made as comfortable as possible. I have no qualms about prescribing drugs in sufficient amount and strength to make it tolerable."

He would put her mind to sleep, out of reach of pain but out of reach of reality too. When death came she wouldn't even know it. She imagined the scene. Warren, faithless Warren, at her bedside, indulging in a little theatrical weeping. Doubtless Yolande too would look in. The two of them might find the scene aphrodisiac.

"I know you'll do everything you can, Doctor."

"Meanwhile, there is counseling."

She was tempted, if only to find out what she would be told. Increasingly now, after earthquakes and tornadoes and floods, one read that counselors had arrived to help the victims cope.

"No."

"You've spoken with your priest or minister?"

She had none. She realized that she was not tempted by religion in her extremity. Now was the time to cry out to God for mercy. Perhaps she would have if she had not found in her misfortune an opportunity to settle with Warren and Yolande. Her whole upbringing, the way she had lived her life, the way she had tried to be, cried out against what she was doing. Others would condemn her if they knew. She understood that. Once she had been like them. But now she realized that there was nothing beneath her feet.

Once on a flight to Europe, settled in, enjoying it, her plane had hit a batch of turbulence and Lucy felt terror in her heart. Next to her, Warren went on reading, but he had had three drinks before boarding and wine with his meal besides. It was surprising he was even awake. She gave no outward indication of her fear, almost no one did. The attendants continued to wear their broad meaningless smiles. Suddenly it occurred to Lucy that this massive piece of machinery weighing tons and tons was hurtling along at nearly forty thousand feet and she was inside it. Beneath her feet were the baggage compartment and then the skin of the plane and a forty-thousand-foot drop she would never survive.

The turbulence had passed, the flight resumed its smoothness, and like the others, she forgot her fear. Now that flight seemed a metaphor of life. The turbulence was a warning, and one that everyone quickly forgot.

Her actions made sense in the world of nothingness she now inhabited. Louis XVI, the last Bourbon king, had cried, "After me, the deluge." He knew he was doomed, his house was doomed, and had said in effect, to hell with it all.

Alma called to ask if she would be going to Michigan City the following day.

"I forgot all about it."

"I was hoping you were driving."

Alma was a former nun who had left her order when she was in her forties, finding it not at all what she had entered as a young woman. Why had she left?

"To be a Christian."

By which she meant visiting the sick and imprisoned, clothing the naked, and burying the dead. Lucy felt a twinge of fear at the thought of Alma burying her. But it was the prospect of a final chat with Lorenzo that decided her.

"Where should I pick you up?"

"You hadn't intended to go, had you?"

"I'm glad you reminded me."

"So am I."

Alma's car was on the fritz and public transportation to the prison was almost impossible. Trains were scheduled for Chicago commuters, not for benevolent ladies who spent a day with prisoners. Lucy jotted down the instructions Alma gave her and put down the phone.

With closed eyes, calmly, she thought of the arrangements she had made. The day after tomorrow she would be struck by a lethal dart fired from a car parked somewhere between Lasalle and Jefferson. She would feel almost no pain, and then would come nothingness.

In a letter she would send to the police she would say that Lorenzo White, aka Rinso, on death row in Michigan City, had told her that Philip Crowe had been hired by her husband to assassinate her. Lorenzo would not quite bear her out, though he might allow that he had mentioned Crowe to Mrs. Flood. Crowe when apprehended—she would provide such leads as she had—would eventually confess to having been hired by Yolande.

If Dr. Lodge then made known her fatal illness, it would be clear that neither Warren nor Yolande had known, so it would be only an ironic flourish to the story.

She could admit to herself that she was amazed at what she had done, and in so short a time. Part of her doubted that it could possibly turn out the way she had planned. "Nothing ever does," Lorenzo said. "Planning is everything, only it ain't enough. You need luck. And God's gotta be with you."

"God?"

69

"The Man." He pointed upward.

"You believe in God?"

"The question is, honey, does he believe in me?"

Well, blacks were naturally religious, weren't they? Even so it seemed strange to think God would be helping Lorenzo waste people, as he so vividly put it.

Lucy was glad Alma had called. Visiting Lorenzo White seemed a good way to spend her penultimate day on earth.

Ten

"You want me to assign someone to watch a pay phone?"

Phelps spoke as if the kind of investigation Warren Flood usually employed him for made a helluva lot more sense. But by and large it was a matter of keeping an eye on an employee suspected of dealing with the competition or, slightly more interesting, gathering evidence for a divorce. Once it had been the runaway child of a client and Phelps had run up an enormous bill which the client was happy to pay just to have his kid back home again to spit in his eye.

"It's more complicated than that," Warren said.

"It better be."

Phelps was a dapper man of perhaps five feet nine. The wings of his collar were held together by a glittering pin, his tie was clasped to his shirtfront by another pin, his wrist when he raised his hand looked like that of a hustler in Naples, displaying a collection of watches. The detective's wrist was shackled with half a dozen gold chains. Phelps avoided backlighting since this revealed how thin his hair was. For a week he had worn a toupee, pretending it was meant as a disguise, then gave it up because it fooled no one.

"I can tell one a block away," he had admitted to Warren.

"You're a detective."

"Anyone could."

"What do you think of mine?"

Phelps leaned forward, squinting at Warren's hairline. His

71

head turned several degrees but his eyes remained on Warren. "Naaah."

"Just kidding."

"Ho ho," Phelps said mirthlessly.

"A client of mine thinks his spouse has contacted a hired assassin."

Warren laid it out for the private investigator; it turned out that Phelps had friends at the local cellular telephone agency. Warren gave him Lucy's number, though not of course telling him it was his wife's.

"The next time she calls this number, they'll call me," Phelps said. "You want to have the police in on it?"

"On what charge? Calling a public phone?"

"You're the lawyer."

"I want photographs of him on that phone. And then I want a tail on him."

"This could be dangerous."

"My client can afford it. But be reasonable."

"If I was reasonable would I be in this kind of work?"

Warren knew that Phelps was in that kind of work because he hadn't passed the bar exams.

"I guess I was too honest for the law," he had ventured once.

"What's that got to do with bar exams?"

"I didn't cheat."

Once he had accepted the assignment, Phelps swung into action. On his first call, he said, "You might have told me it was your wife's phone."

"Does it matter?"

"You can ask that?"

He should have known that Phelps would check out Lucy. The results were startling.

"She's a regular Florence Nightingown," Phelps said.

"Guess who she writes letters for on death row in Michigan City."

"Tell me."

"A hired gun named Lorenzo White. You suppose that's where she got the idea?"

"I don't know." Of course that had to be it.

Phelps had a man in a truck monitoring calls from the house. He passed on to Warren the call from Alma. He was surprised that Lucy was going back to the prison, but his main reaction was relief. If she was still making arrangements there was more time to stop her.

"Who do you know in Michigan City?"

"The prison?"

"The town."

"Why?"

"There was an incoming call from Michigan City to your home this morning."

"Lorenzo?"

"Someone saying her alterations had been made. That must have been a code. She was instructed to call the pay phone at the mall within an hour."

"When was this?"

"Ten thirty this morning."

"But my God, it's noon."

"There are three of them, the hitman and a young couple. They cleared out that phone and were waiting when she placed the call."

"What was said?"

"It'll take place in forty-eight hours. The day after to-morrow."

"Thursday," he breathed.

"Any significance in that?"

"It's my golf day."

After Phelps' call, Warren stared out the window of his office, but what he saw was within. It was incredible to him that anyone, let alone his wife, might wish him harm. It was beyond his imaginative powers to see Lucy calmly going about planning his death. His mind did go back to a dinner at the club with the Kramers. How removed from the company Lucy had seemed, not only remote but also judging Yolande, and not favorably. Warren had often gotten that look from her during a social evening, and felt an anticipation of her later account of how he had behaved. But that was the usual stuff of marriage, wasn't it?

"Why on earth did you go on about your brilliant legal career, Warren? No one cares."

These were remarks a wife was permitted to make in her endless effort to turn her husband into something more presentable than he had been when she took him on. But such judgments were fundamentally benign, made out of the sense that whatever one of them did or said implicated the other. Two in one flesh. An intake of air that was almost a sob. If there had been children, her disciplinary instincts could have been directed at them and she would have been more inclined to take him as he was. Was that it? Now he saw it wasn't. She hates me, he said to himself. She hates me.

But why should anyone, let alone Lucy, hate him? He wasn't large enough to hate. Annoyance, disappointment, genuine dislike for this or that, okay, but hatred? Wanting him dead?

Of course he was dodging what had to be the reason. She had found out about Yolande. That would not have been difficult to do. Once after a trip to San Diego she had questioned an item on their credit card bill, which could have opened a can of worms, but she didn't pursue it. That had been a masseuse. He hadn't even asked her name.

"Paula was telling me today that you have to mo credit card bills carefully. She has found several items that neither of them could account for, and when she complained they were stricken from the bill."

It would be like Lucy to couch her warning indirectly. But if she had learned about Yolande, perhaps told about it by Paula or someone like her, she could never dismiss it. The thought that she might countenance what he and Yolande were doing was repugnant to him. It was rotten and stupid, and he would be more than happy to admit it. It occurred to him that he could plead helplessness. Unable to extricate himself from Yolande, he had become increasingly reckless in the hope and expectation of being caught so that the affair might end. It was the plea of a weak man, but it could work. It was the sort of thing the defense used in serial killer cases.

He picked up his phone and dialed Yolande.

"Something has come up."

"Don't be vulgar."

"Yolande, I'm serious. What are you doing now?"

Meeting at the club seemed best. It would look as if they had just run into one another. He would be in his suit and tie and street shoes; she would be in her tennis outfit. They ordered a drink on the great cool veranda where only older members sat.

"Lucy is making arrangements to have me killed."

She looked at him as if she had been struck deaf and had been unsuccessful in reading his lips.

"She has contacted a hired assassin, someone she probably learned about during her prison visits."

"Lucy did what!"

Their lemonade came and he signed for it. This end of the veranda was screened and the sun lay softly upon the mesh.

From the course drifted the scent of mown grass, birds came and went in the hedge just outside, and the sweet promise of summer was all about. With the tart citric taste of lemon on his tongue, he told Yolande as clearly and calmly as he could what he had learned.

"I don't know if it includes you or not."

That was gratuitous, but he wanted to erase from her eyes that look of phony concern for him. He could imagine himself reacting similarly to her story that Max had hired an assassin to do away with her. Insofar as it left him untouched, he could have almost savored the horror.

"Me?"

"You must see what her motive is."

Her orange lips parted, but she did not speak. She turned toward the screen. The eighteenth green was not twenty yards away. The fairway rose precipitously to the hole so that the final approach was blind. As they sat there, balls appeared on the horizon then dropped back, short of the green. Now what must have been a scuffed shot came sizzling over the hill and onto the green, but kept rolling through until it found the sand beyond. Warren could have cried out for the lost time when making a reasonably good golf shot had seemed the highest moral task.

"What are you going to do?"

"I have a detective on it."

"You've told the police?"

"He is a private investigator. The firm has used him. He's reliable."

She leaned forward and her tanned breasts seemed only uninteresting fatty mounds. "Reliable? I don't care if he's reliable. She has to be stopped."

"Of course."

"How?"

76

Out of dread and fear, out of pique that Yolande should react to this as if it were his doing, came a surprising thought, wrapped in a comforting cliche.

"The best defense is a good offense."

"What does that mean?"

He picked up his lemonade, sat back in the wicker chair and crossed his legs. "Think about it."

"Tell me." She spoke with her teeth clenched. Ah well, she was nervous. His inspiration had brought on a comprehensive calmness.

"What would we do if Max were doing this?"

"He wouldn't!"

"Neither would the Lucy I thought I knew. My point is, if he did, we would act first."

"You think we should kill Lucy?"

Warren gave her a look. Mrs. Dudley was the closest one to them on the veranda and she wore hearing aids in both ears, without noticeable effect. But they had to be careful. How many cases have turned on a remark someone overheard?

"We get someone to do it."

"Do you know such a person?"

"We could outbid her with the man she has."

Yolande took off her straw picture hat and placed it on the table. He saw that she too was calm now. This was a little like playing bridge.

Eleven

Not passing the bar exams was the best thing that ever happened to Phelps, even if it had happened four times before he began to reconsider his options. His position with the biggest firm in South Bend terminated with his first failure. It would have been too demeaning to settle in as a clerk, little more than a paralegal, so he spent a year or two as a broker, feeling like the bank clerk who shells out money all day but has little of his own. Phelps acquired a deep distaste for wealth, when it was in hands other than his own. It had been old Farley, the senior partner in the firm in which he briefly held a position, who suggested that he become a private investigator.

"Our firm could use a discreet man, a man of integrity and honor." Farley had known Phelps' uncle and had an exaggerated estimate of the young man, as he then was.

"You mean like divorces?"

A pained look crossed Farley's face. "You and I do not approve, Stephen, and there is nothing more tragic than a broken marriage. But the law permits it, and we are lawyers. Alas, much of what I have in mind does fall into that category."

Like 99%. Phelps did several inquiries before he got a license, something Farley took care of through powerful friends. Phelps regretted never having known the uncle who had elicited such admiration in Farley. Farley's custom gave the new private investigator eclat and soon other firms were calling on Phelps. Within ten years, he had a suite of offices in the same building as the Farley firm, an office manager, two secretaries, a computer freak and five assistants. With affluence had come delegation, and there were times when Phelps missed being out on a case, shadowing some unsuspecting spouse, taking pictures with a long distance lens, tapping phones, the whole gamut of shady activities that made up his profession. If anything was likely to call him personally into action it was a job for his old firm.

Warren Flood had joined the firm when Phelps already had his bar exams unsuccessfully behind him. It was forgivable, perhaps, if Phelps thought of Warren as the lawyer he was meant to be. It wasn't that Warren had more money, but he had social acceptability. Because of his profession, Phelps was unlikely to be asked to join the country club. Perhaps the committee had the uneasy sense that they might have been the object of his clandestine observation at one time or another. To such suggestions, Phelps simply looked wise. Discretion and confidentiality were the hallmarks of the Phelps agency.

Billie the office manager bumped the call from Warren to him as per instructions. Phelps guessed immediately that the woman Warren was concerned about was his wife. Phelps had admired the aristocratic Lucy from afar, the fine line of her profile, the pinch in the flesh above her nostrils, the lustrous silvery blonde hair. She was a very attractive woman, but one whose function for Warren—this was Phelps' guess based on years studying the darker side of human nature— was a notch or two above his Mercedes. He was saddened to think that there was a fissure in this marriage, but hardly surprised. Of course word of Warren's hanky-panky with Yolande had come to him.

It was one of the minor mysteries of life that the favorites

of fortune gamble away their advantages. Yolande was a play-
mate, a pneumatic body aglow with shallow desires. That one
should want to tumble with her in the hay was understand-
able, but to make a habit of it was insane—for a man like
Warren Flood, that is. Of course Phelps didn't for a minute
believe that Lucy had hired someone to get rid of Warren.

Until he observed the happenings at the pay phone in the
mall.

The trio would not have attracted any attention taken one
by one. The older man could have been a conductor on Am-
trak, a minor official at a bank, an airline navigator. His
manner, his dress, suggested anonymity, someone predes-
tined to be a member of a crowd. The girl was standard
American waif, doubtless sexually precocious, emotionally
immature, full of resentment and hope. The young man, boy
really, Phelps might have seen as a disaster about to happen.
But however nondescript each unit was, when they added up
to three Phelps knew immediately that these were the ones he
was waiting for. He was set up in a shoe store across from the
phone bank and had asked mall security to train their surveillance cameras on the scene as well. Andy at Cellular-You
would record the message.

The fanfare of hustling the fat girl away from the phone
disappointed Phelps. He had expected better of this operation. But then the older man took over and things quieted
down. The leader waited patiently for the ring and answered
it without delay.

He did more listening than talking and when the call was
completed headed immediately out of the mall with the two
youngsters following several paces behind. If he hadn't
known better, Phelps might have thought there was no con-
nection between the three. Outside, Phelps made sure that
his men knew that all three were to be under twenty-four-

hour surveillance until he called it off. Ahead of him lay the puzzle of the taped conversation.

Surprise number one, when he listened to it, was that Warren had it all wrong. It was his wife, not him, who was marked for death. The second surprise was that the woman on the phone could not have been the proposed victim. That it was Lucy's cellular phone number that was used was true enough, but the woman on the line had arranged for the death of Lucia Flood two days hence. Suddenly, the whole situation looked different, and Phelps asked himself what he should tell Warren. A man who suspected that his wife had arranged to have him killed had to be told that it was his mistress who was arranging for the death of his wife. For the moment, Phelps resolved to give Warren minimum information. He could not get rid of the annoying suspicion that Warren was using him in some way he did not understand and sure as hell did not like.

What if a man wished to free himself of a cloying mistress? Might he not put a bug in the lady's ear that the wife must be removed from the scene and pretend to go along with her? Next, employ a friendly and trusting private investigator, saying that it was his wife who was seeking to have him killed. Calls are monitored, investigator reports to husband what the mistress is up to, and he, feigning surprise, insists on sounding the alarm and bringing in the police with the result that the mistress is off his hands and he and his wife are brought together again.

Pure speculation. He called Warren.

"You saw the man she hired?" Warren asked, as if that were the main point of the exercise.

"We have stills and a selection of video recordings, mine and mall security's."

"Who is he?"

"His name is Philip Crowe."

"He's a hired assassin?"

"If he is, nobody knows about it."

"But why would she have gotten in touch with him if he isn't?"

"What was your theory before? The inmate she befriended at Michigan City?"

"That has to be it."

Phelps couldn't figure Warren out. Either he was cunning beyond belief or the stupidest sonofabitch in town. Stupid he wasn't. He would not have risen to a partnership in Farley and Fothergil at all, let alone as quickly as he had, if he weren't very shrewd indeed. Lucy had gone to Michigan City once a month for slightly more than a year, hardly a basis to get on good terms with any inmate. Prisoners are expert manipulators of those who express sympathy for their plight, but they don't really trust civilians. Warren on the other hand had professional reasons as well as opportunity to visit the state prison. Phelps, without any need to do a check on it, thought of the Harter case.

Harter had been tried and condemned, fair and square, and sentenced to be executed, the point at which, as every lawyer knows, circus time begins. Appeals, delays, stays of execution, all-night vigils by whackos who think that all killers need is tender loving care. Once this begins it can continue for years with the rising danger that the condemned will die of old age before sentence is executed. Warren was not brought into the case by Harter, but by a group of the man's friends, animated by his wife, who was absolutely convinced that Harter was innocent. For several months, Warren had been a constant visitor to the prison. He obtained, against the desire of his client, a retrial and in a dramatic moment it emerged that all along Harter was convinced he was taking the rap for his wife, thinking that she had fired the fatal shot. In the course of reconstructing the scene, to bring home the innocence of his client, Warren had done such a vivid job that sobbing suddenly broke out in the court room and a repentant cousin stumbled toward the bench to confess that it was he who had accidentally fired the shot.

In the course of that prolonged effort, Warren could have learned of hired assassins that Harter had encountered in prison. Sheer surmise of course, but Phelps found it a far firmer basis than anything that could be imagined for Lucy.

"Philip Crowe," Warren repeated. "I don't think I ever heard of him."

"Well, after all, how many hired killers have you heard of?"

"Good point. You have someone following him?"

"Around the clock."

"Update me on that, will you?"

"Now?"

"Of course. What did you say I have, forty-eight hours? I want to know all about the guy who plans to kill me."

"You're paying for it."

If Phelps had thought this ambiguous remark would get a reaction from Warren, he was disappointed.

He assigned himself the task of talking with Yolande Kramer at her home, introducing himself and then adding that he was engaged in some investigation work for the Farley and Fothergil firm.

"Oh?"

"More specifically, for Mr. Warren Flood."

She sat back on the couch, as if having second thoughts about giving him a glimpse of her magnificent bosom, and looked at him with narrowed eyes.

"I think I know what you're working on."

"Ah. That makes my job easier."

"Your job is to see that nothing happens to him." She spoke with sudden passion.

Phelps was amazed that even so shallow a woman as Yolande Kramer could prefer Warren to her own husband. Doubtless his amazement was due in part to the fact that he had personal knowledge of Warren, while Max Kramer was an almost mythical figure, a man whose open-heart surgery practice had grown astronomically as the success of his operations became more widely known. Kramer was everything one wanted in a doctor—highly skilled, unselfish, seemingly with but a single motive, the health of his patients. On the other hand, what had Kramer ever seen in someone like Yolande? The question answered itself, of course. No man is immune to voluptuous plenty in a woman. It must be like going to bed with the Naked Maja.

"We monitored the phone call."

She showed no curiosity in this.

"Have you identified the man?"

"Yes."

"Has he been arrested?"

"What for? Indecent phone calls?"

"You mean he's just running around free?"

"He's not under arrest."

"Do you know where he is?"

"That's my job."

"And you report to Warren."

"Yes. I wonder if you could give me any leads in this matter. It's one thing to stop Warren from being killed . . ."

"That's the main thing."

"But we also have to know what the motive was."

"Oh, motives are easy. Women get bored, you know. Are you married? No? Maybe that's best, at least for a man. Men find it easier to be loyal than women do. I suppose I'm a traitor to my sex to say it, but we're fickle. We are. Give us a little attention and immediately we begin to yield."

She swayed toward him as she spoke, and Phelps half hoped he would have to catch her before she fell. Meanwhile, he tried not to stare at the amount of her that emerged from the cornucopia of her gown. He was beginning to understand Warren better all the time.

Twelve

He thought he'd killed the kid in the airport parking lot, and he should have snuffed the girl when he had the chance, but for now Crowe was willing to play master to Larry's apprentice. The girl was just a bimbo, along for the thrill. He kept telling himself that. There had been moments, like when they left the airport and took the cab to the motel, like when he waited for her to finish in the shower, like when the fluttering towel seemed to hang motionless in the air while in the unfocused background she stood naked. And then the mad unvoiced hopes he had in the shower . . . Throughout all that, Crowe had found the icy heart he cultivated, particularly on jobs, begin to melt.

When that jerk at the bus counter called her his daughter, it should have been over. So she was younger than he was, a kid. He had missed a lot of good years, being on the inside and all, and he had making up to do. Only he had never been much with girls. Not when he had to talk to them. Madeline's frailty appealed to him. He didn't want a big beautiful competent woman who would make him feel ill at ease. He wouldn't last five minutes with such a broad. But Madeline needed looking after. She had become involved in something she couldn't really understand. She seemed to think that danger was make-believe. Didn't she realize he had meant to kill Larry when he whacked him with the butt of the gun in the parking lot?

As soon as Larry came onto the scene, Crowe was cured. Forget all the bullshit about her being different, just a fragile little kid who needed Crowe to protect her. Sure she did. She set him up like a pro and took his gun in the bargain. If the two of them had just taken off then the chances of his finding them were slim. Oh, he would have found them. It would have been the point of the rest of his life to show them they couldn't fool around with Phil Crowe and have the last laugh.

"You wanna do what I do?" he said to Larry, as they drove away from the mall.

"That's right."

"What do I do?"

"You know."

"What I know and what you know are two different things."

"Lorenzo told me."

"I doubt that."

"He told me about himself."

That was a point. Of course Lorenzo wasn't going anywhere, not ever, so what did he have to lose?

"Do you hate people or something?"

"Do you?"

"We're talking about you."

"I like money."

"Does Lorenzo look like he made a lot of money?"

"He made money."

"He told you that too?"

"That's right. And I know where it is."

"Sure. In his imagination."

"He said if you talk to him he'll tell you what he didn't tell me and together we can get it."

"Lorenzo always was a generous guy."

"It would be payment for taking me on."

How dumb did the kid think he was? Well, after the way he'd let the girl lead him around, they had a right to think he was stupid. But Larry seemed genuinely interested in learning the trade. Why else had they followed him to the motel in Michigan City, enabling him to get his gun back? He felt like putting the weapon in a weighted nonbiodegradable container and sinking it in the St. Joseph River. With the gun, any prosecutor could not only put him in the row with Lorenzo, he could make a media name for himself. That gun was connected with one unsolved killing after another. Why would these kids have stayed with him if Larry didn't mean what he said?

By God he better mean it, because that was going to be the instrument of Phil Crowe's revenge.

"When do you want to start?"

"Right away."

"All right. You're on. Where's your weapon?"

"I'll get one."

"Where? Did Lorenzo say he'd stashed one away for you somewhere?"

"I'll get one."

"Don't forget, there's a waiting period now."

"Do you think I'm dumb enough to buy a gun?"

"I know you were dumb enough to try stealing mine."

"That was Madeline."

"Geez," she said. "It was an inspiration. Spur of the moment. I didn't mean anything."

Again he felt an involuntary twinge. She hadn't meant anything when she was sweet talking him in that airport motel either. But at the time he'd thought she meant it and he had liked it, he had liked it a lot. Even now, the beauty of the scheme that had come to him was that it would take Larry out of the picture. What would she be like if there were no Larry to run back to?

"So go get one."

"Now?"

"We got work to do within forty-eight hours."

The kid lit up like a video game. He scrambled to his feet, hitched up his pants, and avoided looking at Madeline.

"Any advice for me?"

"Sure. Don't get caught."

And Larry was gone. Madeline came and sat on the arm of his chair. "Are you just funning with him?"

"How do you mean?"

"He's dreamed of this for months, ever since his uncle put the idea into his head. Don't play any tricks on him."

"You want me to turn him into a killer?"

"That's what he wants."

"And you could like a killer?"

She ran her finger from his wrist to his elbow. "I like you."

"Cause I'm a lady killer?"

She held his eyes and then, staring at him until his eyes went out of focus, she leaned toward him and brought her lips warm against his forehead. He tipped back his head and her lips slid wetly down his nose and onto his mouth. Crowe pretended that she loved him, that she was showing her affection and honor and respect. He wanted to believe that, but of course he knew she was just smoothing the way for Larry. She was doing that pretty good.

"Does he know how serious this is?" he said, holding her loosely as she slid down onto his lap and put her arms around his neck.

"I wonder."

"It's not a game. You kill someone, you forfeit your life. Those are the stakes, so maybe it is a game, but a deadly one.

If you get caught, you don't whine and say you didn't mean it. Look at Lorenzo."

"I don't know Lorenzo. I know you."

He made his speech despite the distractions. She had to understand that Larry stood to lose his life and she stood to lose Larry. She said that, yes, she understood that.

"I don't want you coming around in the future telling me you didn't understand."

"Hey, Larry can handle himself."

"Can you?"

"I got you for that."

They did it, sort of, right there in the chair. Madeline did most of the work. What hit him was how casual it was, not that big a deal after all. He hadn't had the time or inclination to wonder if he could. He felt like a goddam bantam rooster and wanted to prance around the room. She was the prize he and Larry were fighting for, and Crowe didn't intend to lose. Losing was not in his repertoire.

You couldn't really say he was setting the kid up by planning to pin it on him. Larry wanted to kill someone, and by God he was going to. And then he was going to pay the price for such a fundamental breach of the laws of society. He wanted to be an apprentice? Okay. Only he would never become a master, because this first try was going to be his whole career.

Larry was back in two hours, all smiles. He had his weapon, a .45, brand new, and for a while Crowe had the sinking sensation that he had used fake ID and bought it himself, establishing a nice link between himself and the clerk, but that made no sense because of the waiting period.

"I noticed there was a Service Merchandise store at the mall. They sell guns, mainly rifles, mostly BB guns, but they have handguns. What do you think of it?"

"So how'd you get it?"

"A guy came to pick his up. Put it in the trunk of his car and then went back inside."

Madeline looked with bright eyes to Crowe for his reaction.

"Good," he said. "Very good."

It was going to be important not to underestimate Larry. He was resourceful. Yeah, that was the word. Resourceful.

Thirteen

As long as the two of them didn't start fighting, Madeline liked the way things were. Crowe was hard to figure out, he said so little and gave away so little when he did talk. His face could be up there on that mountain with those presidents. Mount Rushmore. Pictures of those huge heads just sticking out of the mountain had given her nightmares when she was a kid. Where was the rest of them? Why were they stuck together like Siamese twins, or quadruplets, or whatever? Like the stone heads in that comic strip *B.C.*

"What's it mean?" Larry had said.

She thought he meant the strip she'd shown him, the little guy behind a rock, a psychiatrist. It was so obvious, explaining it would have been hard. But he meant the name of the strip. *B.C.*

"I don't know."

"You don't know."

"Do you?"

"You're the one who shows it to me. I ask what's it mean. Isn't that a reasonable question?"

"You know what your problem is, Larry?"

"Sure, I have an inquiring mind. I like a song, I want to know the words, what the title means."

"You're a pain in the ass."

"Well, I have an inquiring ass too."

"Get your slimy hands off me."

"I'll tell you what *B.C.* means."

"You don't know."

"I'll whisper it."

She twisted away. She didn't want to know. She felt like an idiot, reading *B.C.* for years and not even wondering what it meant. It spoiled reading the strip for her, even after she found out what the title meant.

"That is no longer the approved way of referring to dates," the librarian told her. She was flat as a paper doll and had very white upper teeth that got in the way when she spoke. "When everyone was a Christian, it was different, but now we are more sensitive to our Jewish and Muslim fellow citizens, as well as to those without religious beliefs."

Her voice hummed on, dulling the edge of the small pleasure Madeline felt in getting the answer. She was glad she hadn't told Larry what she thought it meant, something to do with electrical current. He would never have forgotten that if she had said it. It had been far better to be just plain dumb, not knowing, rather than stupid, having the wrong answer.

"He's like a monk," Larry said of Crowe.

"What do you mean?"

"Total dedication. Notice how little he eats. No television. You could walk through the room naked and he wouldn't bat an eye."

"Thanks a lot."

"You want to test him?"

"I'd rather test your handgun on your head."

"Don't say that. It still hurts where he whacked me."

She felt his head and wondered if the lump should still be that big. "It can't be a brain tumor."

"Why not?"

"No brain."

They were wrestling like kids when Crowe came in. He

stepped over them. Larry pushed himself to the wall and sat with his back against it.

"We all set?"

Crowe looked at him. "How can we be all set when we haven't talked about one goddam detail yet?"

"I'm ready."

"I hope so. You ever shoot a .45?"

"In the Marine Corps."

There was silence. "When was you in the Marine Corps?"

Madeline was surprised Larry had brought it up. When he had told her, his lip trembled and he had cried like a baby so she put her arms about him. He'd been given a dishonorable discharge. He had been tops in his platoon, first in all the platoons that went through boot camp when he did. He shot expert at the rifle range, and carried the pylon when they marched for the general on the reviewing stand the day they graduated from boot. He was so gung-ho he didn't even go home on boot leave, hanging around San Diego with a corporal who had been assistant DI for his platoon. One night in the slop chute he learned that he couldn't hold alcohol. A fight broke out, and he was in the thick of it. He ended up in the brig and at office hours he was accused of using racial slurs. That a kid just out of boot camp should call a black sergeant with a chest full of battle ribbons such names was too much for the board. They recommended court-martial, and he was out of the corps in disgrace before his career began.

"They showed me how to use a weapon," he had said, stiffening his jaw. "They showed me how to kill. Someday I'm going to look up that black bastard and stuff a grenade in his ear."

His defense was that he thought of blacks the way blacks thought of whites.

"They knew what I meant, but you can't admit that anymore."

"You said that at the court-martial?"

"It's true."

One thing was true, there was no other Marine Corps to turn to. When she met Larry, he was biding his time, waiting. He was sure there was something he was meant to do. Talking with his uncle Lorenzo told him what it was.

"How can he be your uncle when he's black?"

"Is he black?"

"Come on."

"He married my white aunt. Turns out he also had two other wives in different places."

All the stuff about the handgun had been to tease or test Larry. Crowe said nothing about Larry's being in the Marines, but he wasn't going to question a Marine's ability to shoot.

"We're not using a handgun."

"A rifle? No problem." Larry shrugged.

"It's not really a gun at all."

Crowe got it out, in pieces, and put it together. It looked as much like a bow and arrow as a gun. There was a stock, trigger, guard and lock, but what the trigger released was a dart the size of Madeline's little finger.

"Can that kill?"

"Anything that hits the human body in the right place and with the right force can kill. What's a bullet but a bit of lead? But it's not the impact of this baby that's lethal. It's called a stun gun."

Madeline frowned. She was sure she had seen the thing on some animal show on television. The Discovery Channel? "You going to knock her out first?"

"What's in this dart kills immediately and painlessly. I

95

haven't tested it personally. Who has? But that's the claim."

"You're going to shoot a woman?"

Crowe's eyes were cold and remote. "I am going to fulfill a contract. Do a job. You start thinking of people and this kind of work isn't for you."

"Could I see that?"

Crowe handed Larry the stun gun. "You can practice with that and not wake up the neighborhood."

The neighborhood was south of town, the motel looking out of place, right smack dab among the houses and all. The avenue it was located on had once taken Highway 31 through town, but now there was a bypass and the motel no longer looked like a paying proposition.

Larry borrowed a bike from the owner and rode south to open country to practice with the stun gun.

"You really going to let him do it?" Madeline asked Crowe as Larry pedaled off.

"Are *you* volunteering?"

She shuddered. "I don't even like to think about it."

"Just talk about it?"

"Are you really such a block of ice?"

"It's a job."

"Are you rich? Larry says Lorenzo made a lot."

"Making it and keeping it are two different things."

"What would you spend money on?"

"Houses and lots."

Something in his manner, the shifting of weight, kept her mouth shut. But he went on anyway.

"Whorehouses and lots of beer."

"What's it like in a whorehouse?"

He frowned at her. "It's full of pretty girls who know when not to talk."

On cable there was tennis coming in from some place in

Europe and he watched that, or pretended to. Half the time his eyes were closed. She lay beside him, figuring she'd get a nap if he wasn't up to anything else. She fell asleep. A sweet dreamless sleep that seemed to last forever. When she woke up, he had taken her in his arms and was just holding her gently, rocking her like a baby, smoothing her hair. She shut her eyes again. It was nice.

He said he didn't want her along when he showed Larry where it was all going to happen, and she accepted that. He wanted to be protective. Maybe he was a block of ice, but he seemed to like her.

Fourteen

There were some reasons for having an Ethics Board at the hospital, but Max Kramer could think of a lot more reasons not to have one. It was an incredible waste of time, largely because of Father Brim who had studied moral theology and never gotten over it, even after some years as a pastor. Brim specialized in making the simple complex. Max was sure that, given world enough and time, Brim could make a major moral issue out of opening a door. On the other hand, he treated major surgery as largely a technical problem and was guided by the advice of surgeons. But of course the main reason he was there was to protect their asses. How comforting, when trouble arose, to be able to refer to the approval of the Ethics Board that had preceded the questioned deed. No one who saw the board in action would have any illusions about what its judgments were worth.

Max had acquired a long patience in medical school and in practice and as a result, bad pun, he had acquired more patients than he really wanted. He was extraordinarily good and knew it, but in the way he knew the size of his shoes and that his hair was thinning. It was simply a fact. His practice grew because he hesitated to shunt patients off on other men whose skills he graded lower than his own.

Today, what might have been a short meeting, devoted to a paper Brim had written on the contraceptive effects of a new drug—he was particularly adroit in undercutting the teachings of his own church—lurched toward longevity when Lodge raised a general question.

Max groaned inwardly. Nothing was more dangerous than an appeal to the primitive philosophical equipment of the board, and in this respect he included himself. Abstract, ranging questions by definition had no answer, and when you came right down to it, no practical significance. The issues each of them dealt with were decidedly in the middle distance of moral difficulty and far down in the valley from the alpine principles of which Brim seemed to think himself the personal custodian.

Should a physician, a surgeon, allow his patient to have the last word on treatment when that patient was arguably in a weakened state of mind from having heard that such treatment is necessary?

"Are you talking about headaches?" Brim looked around the table with an inviting smile.

"No." Lodge was irked.

Hooter growled, "Then give it some flesh. What's the illness, what are the treatments, what's the difference one way or the other?"

Lodge now seemed relieved at the demand to be specific, which was good. Max admired Lodge more than he did any other surgeon on the staff, and he did not want anything but the most cordial relations between them.

What Lodge had in mind was a patient who, despite regular checkups, had come up with massive metastasis from a melanoma that had been, it had seemed, successfully treated. The cancer was so widespread now surgery was out of the question. There were however, as Lodge need not tell those here, treatments, chemotherapy, that could prolong the patient's life. Not by much, but some. And, so long as no great hope was placed in them, some surgical procedures might also help. The woman said no, she would leave bad enough alone.

"What's the problem?" Brim had removed his glasses and was massaging his nose.

"Is she in a proper state of mind to make that decision?"

"What's the alternative?" Max asked. "Ask her family?"

"Did I say the patient is a woman?"

"Yes."

"That was a slip. She has also decided against getting a second opinion."

"You think you're wrong?"

"I know I'm not. Perhaps if she heard it from someone else too, now that she's prepared for it and it wouldn't come as such a shock, she would think differently about treatment."

"The treatment does nothing toward curing the disease."

"There is no cure as it stands."

Max suggested that it was on the order of painkilling drugs in the final stage of an illness, then wished he hadn't. It was dangerous to feed Brim analogies. Not listening closely himself, he noticed that Lodge seemed to hang upon the theologian's words. Because he did not wish to intrude his religious beliefs—presumably those of his church, with which he frequently disagreed in any case—Brim's answers were always either/or and if/then solutions. Either you are a Kantian or a Utilitarian; if you are a Utilitarian you must balance the good effects of the action against the bad. The course of action that promises more good effects than bad is the one to be chosen. On the other hand . . .

Lodge was actually taking notes. This was new. Max had always assumed that Lodge had the same opinion of their resident ethicist as he did. With malpractice suits a constant threat, they needed the buffer of allegedly professional ethical advice. The judgment of an ethicist. Where the hell had that word come from? It sounded as if it should be pronounced with a lisp. Pokagan, the anesthetist, was momentarily put out by this, but he recovered sufficiently to suggest that an anesthetist was the opposite of an ethicist.

"Alpha is a negative prefix," Brim explained.

"You both put me to sleep."

Groans. Hadn't Lodge joined in the jollying about Brim? Max decided that the problem Lodge had brought up was really weighing on him. He waited for him outside and walked down the corridor with him.

"Speaking as one dumb old surgeon to another, I think there comes a point when we have to respect the patient's choice."

"If it's made with a clear head."

"What's a clear head? I don't think I ever had one. Would anyone get married with a clear head?"

Lodge was a bit shocked. "You don't really mean that."

"Would you like me to talk to your patient?"

Lodge stepped away and looked at Max, chewing his lip as he did. He shook his head.

"There's absolutely no hope?"

"Of a cure? None."

"So there are only different views on how she faces the inevitable."

"What if a month from now, when she's much farther gone, some miracle cure is discovered? How do you think she'd feel then?"

"That's pretty far fetched, isn't it? Tell me more about her."

"I can't."

"Do I know her?"

Lodge's face was a tragic mask. "I wish you hadn't asked me that."

Doctors burn out or go batty. Surgeons who have been merrily wielding a knife for years, suddenly can't stand the sight of the operating room. Rare still but not unheard of was the diagnostician who begins second-guessing himself, unwilling to stick with an explanation. He ends by driving everyone nuts, including the patient. Max clapped Lodge on the back and was startled to be given an answering hug. Breaking away, Lodge hurried away up the corridor and Max stood staring after him.

It was that half embarrassed abraccio more than anything else that kept his mind on the subject of Lodge's patient. It was as if Lodge had wanted to console him rather than the reverse.

Odd. He must know the woman Lodge was talking about, that seemed clear. Suddenly he stopped thinking and just stared at the wall, having what Yolande called an out of body experience. Yolande! Was she Lodge's patient—insofar as so healthy a person could be called a patient? Lodge had reacted oddly to a tired joke about being married and wished Max hadn't asked him the name of the patient.

"Is anything wrong, Doctor?"

He snapped out of it. "I thought I just saw a nurse."

She made a face. "You're blocking traffic."

"That happens whenever I see a nurse."

He didn't feel a damned bit funny. He went to his locker, changed into street clothes, and drove his Lexus out of the staff garage. He felt exactly as he would have if Lodge had told him that the patient they were discussing was Yolande. Lodge had told him as much, within the bounds of doctor patient confidentiality, that is. No wonder the man had been anguished. Normally he would confide in a fellow physician. And normally the husband was assumed to have a right to know of his wife's illness, but abortion had confused that as it had so many other things in medical practice.

Adding to his certainty was the fact that every recent act of Yolande's that came to mind fed the thought that she had recently learned the dreadful news from Lodge. Dinner with

Warren and Lucy the other night had not been what their eve-
nings together usually were.

"Did you find Lucy strange tonight?" Yolande had asked
as they were getting ready for bed.

"In what way?"

"Why do I even ask? You never notice mood changes in
me either."

"Is that like an out of body experience?"

"Don't joke about things like that."

In lieu of religion, Yolande had an unwavering faith in as-
trology, prophecies, flying saucers and her current diet. What
he had in mind was the opposite of an out of body experience,
but somehow Yolande was not in the mood. Looked back on
now, that scene showed a shattered woman unsuccessfully
trying to talk seriously with her birdbrain husband. He could
kick himself for not shutting up and letting her talk.

Horns blasted all around him. The light could not be
greener. "I'm color blind," he shouted back at the inaudible
obscenity of a driver who shot past him when he had cleared
the intersection. How could he make it up to Yolande?

The first thing he had to do was get her to talk about it.
Lodge's account made it clear that she intended to tough it
out. No second opinion, and that meant at home as well.
Sooner or later, she would not be able to conceal it from his
professional eye, but she probably thought there wasn't that
much later left anyway.

Max felt shut out and felt ridiculous for feeling resentful
about it. Should he get down on his knees and say that her
dying was something they must experience together? The
truth was, he understood the instinct to be secretive about the
verdict, to want to just go off and get it over with. That's what
he would do, and he wouldn't think that he was depriving
Yolande of some treat by doing so.

Fifteen

The address that Alma had given her where she could be picked up was a church. Lucy reached into the back seat for her bag and was digging around in it for the slip she'd written the directions on when there was a tap on the window of the passenger seat and Alma smiled in at her. Lucy unlocked the door and Alma got in. "Thanks so much, Lucy. I didn't want to miss."

"I was afraid I'd gotten your directions wrong."

"No. This is it."

"Do you live near here?"

"Yes."

"Alma, I could have picked you up at your door." Had Alma not wanted to be seen getting into this huge expensive car? She smoothed out a square of black silk, beautifully embroidered, and began to fold it.

"I was at Mass."

"Mass."

"Church."

"Ah. What lovely silk that is. Is it a kerchief?"

"A mantilla."

"I see," Lucy said, not seeing at all.

"I wear it in church. Once women always covered their heads in church. St. Paul. Now no one does. Not even nuns."

"Put it on."

Alma hesitated, then unfolded the mantilla and placed it atop her still honey colored hair. She wore her hair pulled back from several directions and pinned, giving the effect of a luxuriant wildflower. The black mantilla, gorgeous in itself, seemed even more beautiful against Alma's hair.

"If I had one, I'd wear it too."

Alma took it from her head and handed it to Lucy. "Here. I have others." She smiled. "They're a weakness of mine."

"Oh, I couldn't."

"Oh yes you can." Alma folded it and dropped it into Lucy's still open bag.

Impulsively, Lucy leaned toward the older woman and kissed her cheek. It was as smooth as it looked.

"Now we're even," Alma said.

Lucy pulled away from the curb. The prospect of the long drive no longer seemed boring with Alma in the car.

"Today's Thursday," Lucy said.

"All day." Alma laughed. "I used to say that to the kids."

"Yours?"

"I never married."

"I can't believe it."

It just came out. But Alma was such a sweet person, a little cluttered and uncared for, maybe. She didn't seem to do much to enhance her looks, but maybe that was her secret. With her coloring, makeup would have been a mistake. The smoothness of her skin at her age was a marvel. She must be in her mid-fifties. Her eyes were green and her brows were fine, not a simple line, but as if pieced together. They gave her a surprised, wondering look.

"I came on the market too late."

"How so?"

"The children I mentioned were my pupils."

"You taught?"

"For nearly twenty years."

"Why did you quit?"

"I left the Order."

"Order?"

"Of St. Francis. I was a nun."

"I can't believe it!"

Alma laughed. "Oh yes, I was."

"When did you escape?"

"Oh, I didn't want to leave."

"Then what happened?" She glanced at Alma, who did not seem reluctant to talk about it. "Did they throw you out?"

"Oh, nothing so dramatic. It had all changed so much, from the time I entered. It just wasn't the same life anymore. I was the same, but it wasn't. We stopped wearing habits, then even the veil was considered too much. Sisters began to think that teaching and nursing were demeaning, ways of putting down women. When we got out of teaching, I became a nurse. There was more and more of that, complaints that we were being exploited. I tried to convince myself that all these changes were for the best, that these were my sisters, this was my life, and I should accept it all. But I couldn't. So I left."

"When you put on the mantilla you looked like a nun."

"Nuns never wore anything so worldly."

"Why did you go to church today?"

"I go every day."

"Every day?"

"Once a nun, and all that. You can take a girl out of the convent, but you can't take the convent out of the girl."

"Did you really like it?"

"Yes."

Just yes. And Lucy believed her. Nothing in her own life answered to what Alma was telling her. She found it incredible that there still were nuns, but if nuns were fighting against their life, more power to them, as far as she was concerned. Not that she thought that they ought to go on being nuns. The point of their protest should be to get out altogether.

"Isn't that a little much, church every day?"

"Is eating every day too much?"

"They're hardly the same."

"Oh, but they are. Don't you know what the Mass is? It's the Eucharist. The bread and wine become Jesus. Food for the soul. That's where the phrase originated."

Lucy was horrified. Someone had once told her that Catholics believed that the bread and wine literally become the body and blood of Christ, so that eating and drinking them is, what, cannibalism? She tried, delicately, to suggest this to Alma.

"You're referring to the gospel."

"Am I?"

"When Jesus said that he would be our food and drink many of those who had been following him left and went away. It was more than they could handle. It is mind boggling."

Lucy could not believe she was having this conversation. That Alma, loveable Alma, should have a head stuffed full of such nonsense was doubly astounding. She was so sensible looking. So nice and kind. She could imagine what Alma's reaction would be if she were given the news that Dr. Lodge had given her.

She realized that, since waking up, she had not allowed her mind to dwell on what would happen tomorrow, and why. No doubt she would talk about it, at least generally, with Lorenzo. Not about her illness. She couldn't talk about that with anyone. Or so she had thought until this moment. Alma, with her apparent common sense despite all these baroque beliefs, now seemed just the person she could talk to.

"A friend of mine got some very depressing news last week. Cancer."

"What kind?"

"It began with melanoma."

"Oh that can be more dangerous than people think."

"Apparently. She went in for a checkup and out of the blue learned that she has only months to live."

"The poor thing."

The words, a standard remark, were spoken so feelingly that Lucy accepted what she had refused until now, the sympathy of another human being.

"She has refused chemotherapy and all the other things that wouldn't help anyway."

"So she's resigned?"

"She has no choice."

"She can choose whether or not to accept it."

"Well, she's made up her mind anyway. She doesn't intend to just wait for the horribleness either."

"What do you mean?"

"If she's going to die, well, why wait? Let's get it over with."

"She told you this?"

"We're close."

"Lucy, you have to stop her."

"Why?"

"You mean that she intends to kill herself?"

"Yes."

"Oh, how dreadful." Alma's voice quavered with sadness. "She must be out of her mind with dread."

"She seemed very calm about it."

"Stop her. I'll talk with her, if it would help."

"Alma, it's her life."

108

"But it isn't. Did she create herself? Did she will herself out of nothingness?"

"She didn't choose to have cancer either."

"She is angry with God?"

"She doesn't believe in God."

"Oh, the poor thing."

The conversation should have repelled Lucy. She thought of people insistently pushing tracts into her hand, of two young men who had come to her door and spoken with consummate confidence on behalf of the Lord. She was old enough to be their mother, or nearly, and they were telling her the meaning of life. The truth was that she did not like religious people. Faith seemed to her the willful blinking of obvious facts. Or an attempt to build an imaginary world on a foundation of unavoidable facts. Like death. She found herself asking Alma if she believed in a life after this one.

"It sounds too good to be true, doesn't it? Pagans once made up arguments to prove it. I'm glad I don't have to rely on those."

"You take their word or someone else's, isn't that about it?" Lucy asked.

"You could say that."

What made the conversation possible, Lucy thought later, was the fact that Alma said what she believed but showed no disposition at all to persuade Lucy of it. Of course she had said she would like to talk to Lucy's friend who had just learned she had cancer.

"Socrates was condemned to die, unjustly, and his friends urged him to commit suicide and deprive the state of its victim. He refused. Ask me why."

"Why?" Lucy asked.

"He said I don't belong to myself. We don't. That's what your friend should think about. Think about it as only maybe true. Either it is or it isn't. Doesn't that give it a 50% chance of being true? If it is and one takes one's own life, he is hurling himself into the presence of God."

"I thought God loves us all."

"But if we don't love him back we're unable to exist in His presence. And what kind of love is it that throws away the gift of life?"

"Is cancer a gift too?"

"If we're mortal the way we die doesn't really alter things."

"So suicide should be all right."

"Accepting death and causing it aren't the same thing." Alma rummaged in her purse. "Do you mind if I smoke?"

"I didn't know you did."

"Nowadays one has to be so furtive about it."

"Go ahead."

"If you'd rather I didn't . . ."

"Let me have one."

"I don't want to corrupt you."

"Is smoking accepting death or causing it?"

Alma laughed. "You think too much."

Had cigarettes ever tasted good? This one certainly didn't. Lucy couldn't remember the taste of burnt paper. She was sure a stalk of hollyhock would have been as enjoyable. But it was like sharing a little ritual with Alma. Maybe they should have mantillas on.

When Lorenzo was brought into the visiting room, he seemed to shuffle as he walked. Had his shoulders always been so stooped?

"Trouble," he answered when she asked why he looked so low. The chair scraped on the floor when he pulled it out, and he seemed to prolong the nerve-jangling sound. He sank into his chair and breathed a tobacco breath across the table. "Real trouble."

"You look healthy," she lied.

"You recall that ole friend of mine we talked about, man who took up where Lorenzo left off?"

"Philip Crowe?" She mouthed the words as Lorenzo had always insisted, not pronouncing them. Was it fanciful of him to think their conversations were monitored?

"That man is at it again, and my little nephew has taken up with him. Now you know it don't do much good for an old sinner like me to tell young people not to be foolish the way he was. They're going to think I'm talking now but I wouldn't have talked that way when I began, and that's true. It's true. We have to do dumb things in order to know they're dumb."

"I don't know if we have to, but it is the most effective lesson."

He wanted her to write a letter for him to this nephew and take it with her when she left. It was important that he get the letter as soon as possible.

"I'll send it Federal Express."

"What's that?"

She explained it to him.

"Good. I'm glad they got that. Send it that way, and I'll pay for it."

"What do you want to tell him?"

Lorenzo was surely right in thinking that the platitudes he dictated would be ineffective with his nephew. She had never told him that she had indeed contacted Crowe. She didn't like the idea that Crowe was involving some child in this.

"How old is your nephew?"

"He isn't thirty years old."

Maybe not a child, but one more person than she had imagined. She felt responsible for the nephew, who had been named after Lorenzo and now imagined he would follow in his uncle's footsteps.

These were not the thoughts she had imagined having, nor the conversation, when she decided to come today. If she had thought of the prison at all, it was as a place she had already seen for the last time, like so many others. Her volunteer work had proved useful in a way she would never have guessed. The first time Lorenzo spoke frankly to her of what he had done, it was like listening to a member of another species. Her trouble had made them more alike than different now.

Talking with Alma had robbed her of the persistent angry awareness of what was happening to her. She had hated Dr. Lodge for telling her, hated the technicians for discovering it, hated Warren because she did not wish to tell him, hated Yolande because of her superficial manner of living—oh, she hated her too for having an affair with Warren, and she had arranged to punish them as well as herself. If there were a God she would have hated him most of all, but it had never even occurred to her that there was. Could she hate the God Alma believed in?

"Do you believe in God, Lorenzo? Really?"

"I do. Yes, I do."

"What's he like?"

"I won't know till I get there."

"But you're sure he's waiting?"

"I'm afraid he's waiting. Sometimes I wished he weren't. I got a lot of explaining to do, but I'll throw myself on the mercy of the court. Except I know what that can get you. So they's days when I think, I'll die and my soul'll come oozing out of my body and then just evaporate. Like smoke. Gone. Just sucked up into whatever's still going on that's not me anymore."

"It's possible."

"It's possible I'll come back as a kangaroo, but I don't expect it."

"I have a friend who believes every word of it."

"Good for him."

"It's a lady."

"Believing's easier for ladies."

"Why do you say that?"

" 'Cause it's true. I've noticed. Go look in most any church most of the time, what you gonna see? Women. And who was there around the cross when all the men got the hell out?"

There was no more point in talking about terminal illness with Lorenzo than there was with Alma. Would it really be simpler if she believed as they did? Nothingness was almost comforting beside the notion of hell.

"Do you believe in hell, Lorenzo?"

"I'd rather not talk about it."

"But you think it's there?"

"It's in the Book. People try to say it isn't, like they say the Book ain't against divorce. But that don't make it so."

It was the strangest day Lucy had been through in a long while, even stranger in its way than when she had heard her death sentence pronounced by Dr. Lodge. The effect of talking to Alma and Lorenzo was that she began to wonder what did await her after her assassin performed his work.

When it came time to go Alma said she wouldn't be going back with her, she wanted to stay on.

"How will you get home?"

"I'll leave in time to catch the train."

"Well . . ." She realized that she had been looking forward to driving back with Alma.

"About your friend? Tell her not to worry. She's going to be all right."

"I told you she isn't religious."

"I mean all right now. Cured. I am going to say some special prayers to Mary. She never fails. Your friend will be cured."

"I can't tell her that," Lucy said, angrily.

"Sure you can."

"Alma, how many times have you prayed for something and it didn't happen? It would be cruel to raise hope . . ."

"It's when you pray for yourself that the answer's usually no. But I'm praying for her. She isn't going to die."

"Oh, Alma."

"It's you, isn't it?"

"Why on earth would you say that?" But Lucy felt that she had told Alma, or that the little woman had known right along who had received the bad news.

"I mean it, Lucy. I wouldn't say it if I weren't confident. Our Lady of Fatima won't say no."

Who on earth was Our Lady of Fatima? Alma took her hand, then lifted her lips to her cheek. Lucy took her in her arms and began to bawl like a baby. And even as she cried she could have struck Alma for saying these things to her when she was so vulnerable. She broke free and hurried out of the building and to her car.

Sixteen

"What's this?" Warren asked, picking up the envelope from the hall table.

"What's what?"

"It's a letter addressed to Lorenzo Donovan."

She came out of the study, glanced at the letter and nodded. "I promised to mail it."

"Promised who?"

"The inmate I help at the prison."

"You were there today?"

"Obviously. Do we have any envelopes and forms for Federal Express?"

"If we do they're on the office account. I hope you didn't intend to mail your prisoner friend's letters that way."

"I told him I would. I suppose I'll have to go to their office. Are they still open?"

"I'll take it down for you."

"Now?"

"Of course."

"Thank you, Warren. That will be a help."

She laid a hand on his arm and went on upstairs. Warren stared after her. Thus Judas had betrayed by kissing the victim. Warren read again the name written on the envelope, then began to slap it distractedly on his arm where Lucy had put her hand. He could see the narrow rat face of the boy whose name this was.

He kept everything Phelps had given him at the office, and he had poured over the still photographs, telling himself that these were the faces of motiveless killers—at least they had no personal knowledge of or motive to kill their victim. It was simply a business proposition. You would like X to disappear from the face of the earth? Fine. That will be so much.

How much? It seemed an indication of what this was doing to him that for the first time he realized that Lucy would have passed on money to these animals, presumably a great deal of money. He had a vague notion what his body was worth, reduced to its component chemicals. What was his life worth to an indifferent wife motivated by anger just because he might be getting some small enjoyment out of an affair with the gymnastic but satisfying Yolande?

"Max is a lucky guy," he had once said to Yolande, his heart slowly regaining its normal beat after their exertions.

"Oh we never do things like that."

"You don't?"

"With my husband? Not on your life. Those are fun things." She began to play his ribs like a keyboard. "Naughty things." She put her tongue in his ear and moved it wetly about and, incredibly, he was rampant again.

The image momentarily blurred his mind. From upstairs, Lucy was calling to ask if he had gone yet.

"Just leaving."

"Wait."

She came down again, in stocking feet, keeping a grip on the railing so she wouldn't lose her footing. She handed him another envelope, sealed, unaddressed.

"Will you put that in with the other?"

"What is it?"

"Money."

"Money!"

"The letter's to his nephew, and then he said he wished he could send him some money. I told him I would."

"How much?"

"Warren, don't ask. I'm being generous, all right?"

She stood with one hand on the newel post, her feet on different steps, a thoughtful look on her face.

"Warren, why don't we believe in God?"

"Don't believe in God? What nonsense. Of course we do. At least, I do."

"You never mentioned it."

"It's not the sort of thing you mention."

"Warren, I've had the oddest day. I seemed, through no fault of my own, to be getting into discussions of religion wherever I went."

"On death row? I'm not surprised. There are no atheists in fox holes."

"What's that mean?"

"What it says."

"What's a fox hole? It's not literally about foxes, is it?"

"A sort of trench, in war time. The front lines, shells coming in right and left, one has your number on it. You've seen the movie."

"I shouldn't think they'd have time to think about such things."

"You'd be surprised."

"That's what I said. Did I ever mention a woman named Alma to you?"

That wasn't the girl's name, if Phelps had got it right. Lucy sat on the stairway and gathered her skirt around her legs. He had forgotten how large her feet were. With the funniest look on her face she began to talk about the woman named Alma, who was a nurse, and before that had taught school.

117

"She used to be a nun."

"You never told me."

"I just found out today. She believes in miracles."

"Loaves and fishes, Lazarus raised from the dead, the blind made to see, the lame to walk?"

She stared at him. "What are you talking about?"

"The New Testament."

"Have you read it?"

"I used to. When I was a kid. Didn't you?"

"I don't remember. But those are old miracles. Alma thinks they go on right now."

"Did they throw her out of the convent?"

Lucy looked at him coldly as she got to her feet. "She was not thrown out. She left. Are you going to mail those things?"

She had delayed him with that nonsense about her friend Alma and then blamed him for not having left. It was the kind of annoyance that seemed almost attractive, the stuff of minor marital strife. He could happily live with that. Don't forget, he reminded himself, that woman has arranged your death.

He gripped the wheel of the car and stared grimly ahead. Two could play at that game, by God. But only one would succeed.

At the Federal Express office he printed a note on the back of a form. UNCLE LORENZO SAYS CALL THIS NUMBER 317 232 2960. He put it in the cardboard envelope provided and filled out the slip, copying the address from the first envelope Lucy had given him. He put that envelope and the money in his pocket and took the packet to the counter.

"I want to send that overnight."

The clerk, a short woman with dark eyes and abrupt movements, nodded.

"Will it get there in the morning?"

"As soon as night is over."

Wit is everywhere. Well, it was a stupid question and one this woman had obviously heard too often. She was a whirl of efficiency behind the counter, one of those rare creatures whose energies are not tailored to her salary. She couldn't earn much doing this; after all, this wasn't the post office.

In his car, he found himself unwilling to wait. Tomorrow was the day! When night was over it might already be too late. He stopped downtown on the way home, signed the book in the lobby and took the elevator to his office. How different the building seemed at night, and so did his office. He felt like an intruder when he sat at his desk. He picked up the phone and asked for the number at the address he read off from the convict's envelope.

"Would you dial it?"

"Certainly."

Somewhere in hell a phone began to ring. Where was the circle of assassins in the Inferno? Odd that Lucy should think he did not believe in God. It was his shame, rather than his boast, given the present course of his life. But his vestigial faith included the conviction that God is particularly merciful toward sins of the flesh. He didn't know what biblical warrant there was for this belief, but it had settled in his mind long ago and rendered possible his continued inner allegiance to the faith of his fathers, despite his sexual shenanigans.

This night thy soul will be required of thee. The verse formed full-blown in his mind, adding urgency to this phone call. He did not want to be hurled into eternity with all his sins upon his soul, like Hamlet's uncle. He would wean himself from Yolande, meaning he would try to dump her without incurring her wrath, and put his house in order. The easy way he had answered Lucy now seemed a judgment on him. Of course he believed in God. But he had no image of the object of his belief. Jesus? There were Arian and Unitarian strains in Warren's belief. God was remote, wholly different. Indifferent too? An abstract and aloof God could hardly be expected to trouble himself with the peccadillos of one Indiana lawyer. He would have better things to do. Besides, think of the billions of people currently teeming on the earth, each with his, or her, faults and sins and blemishes. Warren felt an impulse to wave away the misdeeds of those anonymous masses. It was like giving a blessing before battle, instant forgiveness.

"Hello?" A woman's voice.

"Lorenzo gave me this number."

A pause. "Just a minute."

"This is Lorenzo," a petulant male voice said. Warren could see him from the photographs Phelps had given him.

"Uncle Lorenzo asked me to call. Are you alone?"

"I didn't answer the phone."

"Anyone else there?"

"Who else would there be?"

"Crowe."

A long silence. A hand covered the phone. Warren was in an agony, waiting. Was Crowe there, were they hatching some scheme?

"Who are you?" the kid asked.

"We have to meet tonight."

"Tonight?"

"In South Bend." He was about to give him the address of the building he was in, but the thought of a hired assassin signing the visitors' book in the lobby stopped him.

"I'm not driving all the way back there tonight."

Warren thought wildly. The kid hadn't said no, after all, and he had to at least talk to him and try to throw a wrench into whatever was planned for tomorrow.

"Lorenzo recommended you for a very delicate task."

"Yeah."

"He said you would know what I mean."

"Who are you?"

"You can check with Lorenzo."

The kid snorted. "Just call his private number?"

"Our meeting will be at the first oasis eastbound on the Indiana Tollway. In two hours."

"What's in it for me?"

"More money than you've ever had before."

"Just a minute."

Again a hand covered the phone, and time ticked slowly by. When the hand lifted, the girl was still talking.

"Okay. Two hours from now."

"Is Crowe there?"

"Are you kidding?"

He then called home to tell Lucy he was at the office.

"It was a big mistake to come here. There was an urgent message and when I telephoned the client I had to agree to see him tonight."

"All right."

"I don't know when I'll get home."

"Ah well, a client."

Of course she would think that he had decided on the spur of the moment to be with Yolande. His anger was in direct proportion to the plausibility of her suspicion. It helped to be angry with her. By God, this was the woman who had cold bloodedly entered into negotiations with a paid assassin. He was scheduled to be killed tomorrow, he knew not when or where or how. Did Lucy think she was granting him a last night's fling with Yolande? The truth was he would not have been of much use to her at the moment, attributable, he told himself, to the tension and anxiety felt by a man who knew there was a contract out on him. Warren remembered the pleasure he had derived from watching Charles Bronson and Clint Eastwood in assassin roles. Did anyone ever feel sorry for the target?

He pushed back from his desk and became aware of the envelopes in his pocket. He took out the smaller envelope, studied it, palpated it, then tore it open. The bills inside were crisp and new. Fifty one-hundred-dollar bills. Good Lord. She had said she was being generous, but this was ridiculous. Well, this would do very well as a down payment on the assignment he intended to give young Lorenzo.

Seventeen

Phelps led a dangerous life as lives go but he had never, to the best of his knowledge, been the intended target of an assassin's bullet. He had been shot at three times, once by mistake, the other two times by the objects of his investigative attention, and only one of those had been really deliberate. Still it was a dangerous life. Even so he found it difficult to put himself in his current client's shoes.

When Warren Flood had told him that his wife was arranging for him to be killed, Phelps had permitted himself to feel a skepticism he did not betray. Given the fare on television and in the movie houses of the nation, the most sequestered of housewives was versed in the alleged procedures of the Mafia. In these quickly produced dramas, hired killers were easily available, as if they could be found in the phone book. The threat of hiring such a tradesman might come easily to the lips of Warren's wife.

Particularly when one knew, however much at a distance, as Phelps did, the woman in question. He preferred to think that if Lucy were ever brought to the peak of enraged vengeance she would do the deed herself with some household instrument ready to hand and snatched up unthinkingly. A butcher knife, even a table knife, the poker from the fireplace, any heavy but liftable object around the house. But a planned and prolonged campaign? Phelps preferred to think that with the cooling of passion would come the realization that

Ralph McInerny

Warren was not worthy of such an act on her part.

All this skepticism had been wiped away in a few minutes of surveillance at the mall. Lucy was dealing with the real article. Crowe had no record as a killer, but Phelps had little doubt he was practiced and professional. The tape of the telephone conversation added to this impression.

Harrison had followed the younger one, Larry, into the country where he had practiced with what Harrison called a crossbow.

"You're kidding."

"He got the knack of it really fast. Not a bad idea when you think of it."

"No noise."

"You know what I'd use? A blow dart. The kind the South American Indians use," Harrison added vaguely. "That would be best."

"If you don't inhale."

A lethal dart. Phelps ran a check and found that there had been no deaths in the United States in the past ten years due to poison dart. Well, it obviously wasn't Crowe's MO, on the assumption that he had one. It would be shrewd to vary methods with the case. This choice suggested solicitude for the victim, and that fit in with what he assumed Lucy's instructions to Crowe would have been.

Only it couldn't be Lucy, it had to be Yolande identifying herself as Lucy. Phelps was amazed at Warren's brazenness, in coming to him with the story of Lucy contacting hired killers, when all along it was Yolande. And the target was Lucy. That ruled out any possibility that it was the holder of the cellular phone number, Lucy, making the arrangements. She should pay someone to stalk and kill her? It had to be Yolande. Only if Yolande was doing this without Warren's knowledge did his reaction make sense, but that did not square with his knowing such arrangements were being made. Of course he claimed that he was the intended victim. The situation was confusing enough to make Phelps decide that he personally would keep an eye on Warren.

Phelps had just settled down in a panel truck, ostensibly from the power company, parked half a block away from the Flood home, prepared for anything but expecting an uneventful night, when Warren backed down the driveway. He hadn't been home half an hour; he couldn't have eaten. Phelps scampered into the cab and started the engine, pulling on a cap and prepared to duck should Warren come this way. But Warren went in the opposite direction, pulling to the curb at the Fed Ex office.

Federal Express? Phelps's heart sank. He had no contacts in Federal Express. Of course it was probably wrong to think that this errand had anything to do with the case he was on, though it was hard to imagine Warren just tending to business as the hour of the attack drew near.

Warren came out of the office, carrying a fluttering slip of paper. On the way to his car, he looked at it, thought, then shoved it into a waste paper receptacle. When Warren started down the road to the highway, Phelps hopped out of the truck, ran to the receptacle, got the top off it and reached in. The thing was filled with carbons of Fed Ex forms, but the one on top had to be Warren's. Phelps loped back to his truck and looked down the road where Warren was still being held up by the light.

He started slowly down the road, wanting to be only close enough so that he could goose the truck and make it through the same green light Warren did. He could kick himself for bringing this truck, hardly what he would have chosen as a pursuit vehicle. He glanced at the slip.

Lorenzo Donovan. A Chicago address. The kid who was

working with Crowe. The light changed, he got to the highway and through the yellow and turned left, following Warren downtown.

After Warren had checked in and taken the elevator, Phelps went inside and talked with old Leo who had been night watchman in Phelps's time with Farley and Fothergil and had welcomed him back to the building when prosperity had made renting his own offices here feasible. This also put him close to many of the lawyers who made regular use of the services of Phelps Confidential Investigators.

"Busy night," Leo said.

"Was that Warren just came in?"

"That's right."

Phelps checked his watch. "Right on time." He looked over his glasses at Leo. "Will you do me a favor?"

"What's going on?"

"I wish I could tell you. It's important."

Leo's narrow chest swelled beneath his starched uniform shirt. Phelps told Leo to call him in the garage when Mr. Warren came down. "Just say he's on his way."

"You going to need any help?" Leo hitched his trousers and laid a blue-veined hand on the butt of his revolver.

"I don't think so. I'll tell you when you call."

Parked in the garage was a car more appropriate for following Warren around. Nonetheless, he got into the panel truck where he could monitor any calls Warren might make. As a precaution, he had put a tap on his office phone, but thus far this had produced only information that would have been of great use to his competitors in the law.

Warren's call to Lucy suggested that it was going to be a long dull night. Well, better in the garage than in the street across from Warren's house. But then Warren put through a call to Chicago requesting a telephone number, which of course Phelps jotted down, and then the significant if enigmatic discussion with Larry. Phelps congratulated himself on the hunch that had led him to put in that tap. At the time, it had been motivated solely as a protection of his client. This case was so full of ambiguities it had been difficult to know, or at least to accept, who the intended victim was. Now, it seemed clear, Warren was up to no good at all. It was also clear he could not follow him to the rendezvous with the younger Lorenzo in the panel truck. Fortunately, he had an alternative there in the garage.

Leo rang to say that Warren was on his way. Phelps thanked him in the crisp tones of one who owed a favor.

It was a grim preoccupied Warren who came through the steel fire door into the garage. His heels echoed in the low-ceilinged, eerily lit garage, but if he heard he gave no indication. In his car, he sat immobile behind the wheel for a moment with the look of a man about to do something unlike anything he had ever done before. But then, resolved, he started the motor and moved rapidly up the ramp into the street. Phelps followed at a discreet distance.

Warren turned west, drove the mile and a half out Lincoln Way to the bypass and then took it to the north. Almost immediately he was exiting for the tollway and the westbound booth. Phelps went through a half minute after Warren, punched the button and got his ticket.

The advantage of following another car at night is that the pursuer is not easily detected among identical headlights. The disadvantage is that the pursued is equally anonymous, one set of taillights being indistinguishable from another. Phelps followed Warren very closely, accordingly, not wanting to run the risk of losing him, even if he knew the destination.

Interstate driving was not rendered much less boring because he was on a job, and he was glad when they came to the final oasis. Now he would find how Warren meant to deal with the problem that the first oasis on the toll road east-bound was across four lanes and a concrete divider from the last oasis westbound. Would he now take the next exit and re-join the toll road eastbound? The answer was no. He pulled into the westbound oasis, and Phelps kept close behind him now.

Warren got out of his car and, oblivious to everything else, began to walk toward the toll road. It was obvious what he planned to do, and it seemed indicative of the reckless course he was taking. At the edge of the eastbound lanes, he stood for a moment, a tall silhouette, poised, waiting, then in a lull he dashed for the meridian, went over the concrete wall like a track star and was poised waiting to cross the eastbound lanes by the time Phelps, encumbered by cameras and other equip-ment, got to the first lap. It was a time when he could have lost Warren for sure if he had not known where he was going. The oncoming headlights blurred into a river of brightness, and there was no promise at all of its letting up. Through the passing cars, Phelps could see Warren sprint across the east-bound lanes. He at least had arrived at the rendezvous.

Phelps, muttering profanely, waited for a lull. He was damned if he was going to kill himself. On the other hand, he had not come this far to miss the meeting. Finally, he was able to dash for the meridian, get himself over the barrier and find that the eastbound lanes seemed momentarily deserted. He could have strolled the rest of the way.

He made the near-fatal mistake of going right inside the oasis. Warren was just emerging from the men's room and was on the alert for the man he had arranged to meet. Of course, like Phelps, he knew what the young Lorenzo looked like, though Phelps had the advantage of having seen him in person. Warren's eyes swept unseeing past him, while Phelps held his breath. In a moment, Warren had disappeared into the restaurant.

The restaurant was served by a fast food chain. Warren got in line and squinted at the illuminated menu over the counter. His was the look of one who had not eaten such food before. Meanwhile Phelps went into the kitchen.

"You can't come in here," a three-hundred-pound uniformed girl complained.

"Where's the manager?"

"The manager's not in the kitchen."

Phelps smiled conspiratorially and pulled out the ID he had decided on for the occasion. His voice dropped to a whisper as he explained to the girl that his television station was taping a contestant while he met with someone.

"You ever see Candid Camera?"

She was too young for that. She thought it was his program. Her frown had fled and her interest in his equipment grew.

"I'll need some shots of you at work. All right?"

She was aflutter with excitement now. Phelps hoisted his video cam and ran a few feet of the largest waitress in the world. She was his.

"The point is, he mustn't see me."

The manager came in, and Phelps caught him on video as he was being introduced. The whole place was now at his disposal. He was led to a spot behind a kiddie play area where he had an unobstructed view of the dining room. The manager was at his elbow.

"There he is," Phelps said, pointing at Warren who, with laden tray, was again looking around for Lorenzo. Phelps had already spotted Lorenzo, seated in perfect camera range with the girl. The first shots, after the vanity ones of the now complicit staff, followed Warren going to join the two, introductions all around, hesitation, then a handshake. Perfect.

Once Warren sat down, things moved at Central Glacial Time. But that gave Phelps time to fiddle with his long distance feed. He couldn't hear more than murmuring with the naked ear, but this mike worked marvels.

There seemed to be some confusion in the trio. The girl looked at the boy, they both looked at Warren, but after this initial rough spot, the conversation proceeded smoothly. Phelps would have to wait until he played the video to hear the audio, presuming he was getting it. If not, he would get a lip reader to decode. Warren had taken an envelope from his pocket and placed it on the table, his arched fingers still on it. The girl concentrated on the envelope; Larry's eyes went back and forth like a tennis fan's between the envelope and Warren, who continued to talk. The money, as it must be, worked magic. Ten minutes after he had sat down, Warren was up, shaking hands. He got in the way of the mike then, blocking the view of the others, but presumably the essential business had been done. Mission accomplished. Warren had apparently succeeded in undoing whatever it was Yolande had planned.

If the victim was indeed Lucy. Something was very confusing in this whole business. To take it on its own terms, one had to think that Lucy, a lovely young woman in her early forties, had taken out a contract on her own life. Obviously that made no sense. Number one, she seemed on top of the world and, number two, if she were depressed and wanted out, there were any number of simpler ways to do it. The only possibilities that made any sense to Phelps were two. [1] It was Yolande's take-out that Lucy was arranging, identifying herself as Yolande. [2] The other was that Yolande was arranging for Lucy's death, having learned about killers and the like from Lucy herself, thanks to her acquaintance with such animals as Lorenzo White.

Well, it didn't matter now, since Warren had apparently succeeded in calling off the dogs. His decision to deal with the youngsters, rather than with Crowe, looked inspired. A thought hit Phelps, a lovely possibility that would cause him to revise his opinion of Warren. What if he had arranged for the younger killer to take out the older one? That would explain why he wanted to see him alone. And Warren was lawyer enough to be able to stick the young guy with the killing while looking innocent as the driven snow himself. What a guy.

Warren was now on his way out of the oasis restaurant. Phelps left by way of the kitchen, video cam running as he panned the place, eliciting the usual phony smiles and giggles, and then he was on his way. When he came outside, he could see Warren walking slowly toward the traffic, preoccupied. For a moment he feared he was going to walk right into it, but he stopped, looked casually to his left, then strolled over to the meridian to the anguished honking of the cars that missed him.

Phelps got to his car in time to follow Warren back onto the tollway. Warren took the next exit and then got onto Highway 20 for the drive back. On the way through Michigan City, he was distracted by the Yokohama Spa, slowing as he passed, craning to see what he could see. He circled the block and entered the spa parking lot.

While he was inside, Phelps had a chance to play his tape. Of course it was the sound he was interested in. The images were good, the sound adequate.

Warren: Are you Lorenzo?

Larry: Call me Larry.

Warren: We talked on the phone.

Larry: Yeah.

Madeline: Ask him to sit down.

Larry: Have a seat.

Warren: Does Crowe know you're here?

Larry: Who's Crowe?

Warren: You know who he is.

Madeline: He means Crowe doesn't know.

Larry: [chanting] Crowe don't know, Crowe don't know, Crowe don't know what Crowe don't know.

Warren: He agreed to do something for my wife.

Larry: Not for her, to her.

Warren: What do you mean?

Madeline: Don't you know?

Warren: He agreed to do a job for my wife.

Madeline: You want to stop him you better talk to Crowe.

Larry: You said you had something for me to do.

Warren: I do have another job. [The crinkling sound must have been the removal of the envelope from his pocket] Yolande has a husband.

Larry: Yeah?

Warren: This money is for you to take care of him.

Larry: [the sound of the envelope being opened] We'll call this half.

Warren: All right.

Larry: When you want this done?

Warren: [in a strangled voice] Soon.

Larry: How about tomorrow? We'll be in town anyway.

Warren: Don't joke about it.

Larry: You got pictures or anything?

Warren: I didn't have time. Here is his address.

Larry: Well, okay. I don't want to make any mistakes.

Warren: The girl could find a picture of him in back issues of the local paper.

Larry: Is the girl willing to do it?

Madeline: I'll do it.

Warren [standing]: We have a deal then?

Larry: Any special way you want this done?

Warren: Be swift and painless. I don't want to know any details. You realize I will deny ever having spoken with you.

Larry: Me too.

Phelps sat back. What a sonofabitch Warren was. And Phelps had imagined him meeting these killers in order to call off the arrangements made by Lucy. Instead he had insured that Yolande would lose a husband when he lost a wife. But anger was replaced with grim satisfaction.

For a lawyer, Warren was a stupid ass. Of course he could deny ever having talked to those killer kids. But only an idiot would fail to see that it could not have been by accident that he and Yolande lost the impediments to their permanent liaison at the same time. Phelps patted his camera. There was also the recording of the meeting, something Warren had never counted on.

He left then. Warren must be getting the imperial deluxe treatment in there. Phelps no longer cared what happened to the weasel.

Eighteen

Madeline didn't trust him. And she could see what he thought of Larry, but what real difference was there between them? They were different sides of one handshake. What Madeline noticed was that he didn't seem to give a damn about his wife. After he left, when the money was stashed safely in her bag, she said to Larry, "You're not going to do it, are you?"

"What do you think?"

"I think we should take this money and go."

"Crowe wouldn't like that."

"Crowe has nothing to do with this. It's no skin off his butt if we take this guy's money. He won't even know about it. And how can twinkle toes complain?"

"Twinkle toes?"

"Did you see the way he walked?"

"What are you, queer for feet?"

"Just heels."

She caught his hand, just in case he didn't intend a friendly tap. "Larry, I mean it. Let's go. There's something weird about this whole thing, but this money is real and it's ours."

"We haven't earned it."

"We drove out here and listened to him."

"That's worth five thousand dollars?"

"Is that how much it is? I was too excited to count."

She put her bag in her lap and opened it, and the two of them reached in to count the bills.

"I get fifty."

"Me too. If they're all hundreds it's five thou."

"My God."

A man with a baseball cap was staring open mouthed at them. Madeline lifted her purse to show him where Larry's hand had been. He didn't acknowledge the explanation. Maybe he'd had a stroke. When they went by him, Madeline waved a hand in front of his face. He blinked.

Larry whistled and sang and was generally happy as a lark on the way back to Chicago, but Madeline didn't know what he had decided to do. Dark little thoughts of taking off alone with all that loot came and went. She'd do that rather than hang around with Crowe anymore. She knew, even if Larry didn't, that Crowe had his eye on her. She had given him TLC and led him on and now he was hooked and that was bad news for Larry. The more Madeline heard of the arrangements for the next day, the less she liked them.

"For example, why are you doing the shooting?"

"Because I am learning and he is giving me a break. At this point, it doesn't matter anyway. We're all in it equally, no matter who actually does it. We're all part of the conspiracy." He pronounced it with a hiss, and his brows danced up and down. He reached out and grabbed her knee and began to horse around. She squirmed away.

"I forgot I have automatic transmission."

"I don't want any transmission from you."

They were all part of it, all right, and she didn't like it. The truth was she trusted neither of them, Crowe because he was a killer and hated Larry, no matter what he said, and Larry because he was such a kid around Crowe. In school there had always been boys like Larry, sucking up to the bully, hoping some of it would rub off on them. Larry was still like that. He would always be like that. Only Crowe was a killer. The time he told her she was dead, under sentence of death, she had believed him. The sentence had never been lifted either. So what was he up to?

He didn't need Larry. Larry was an impediment rather than a help. So why did Crowe keep him around? It was nice to think it was because of her, but there was no point kidding herself. Of course he liked it, all men do, but that didn't mean she had any claim on him. Madeline became certain that it was Crowe's plan to kill them both in the end, Larry and herself.

"He kills for money," Larry said.

"But you're doing the killing."

"We work together."

What a dope he was. He acted as if he had gotten back into the Marine Corps, a second chance, and this time he was going to do it right.

Nineteen

He had never, Max realized, considered Yolande to be quite grown up and this rendered his task more difficult. When she had said she did not want children, not yet, he did not insist. To imagine her as a mother required an effort he was unwilling to make. No more did he expect her to keep household accounts or remember to have her car taken in for regular maintenance or notice when something around the house, an appliance, a fixture, showed signs of needing attention. All these things he took care of. It would have been nice to have her do it, but after all she was Yolande, beautiful, affectionate, immature.

How could he talk to her of life and death?

Everything she said and did now took on a significance it would not otherwise have had. Her cheerfulness, modified by a constant claim to being bored, seemed heroic in the circumstances. After dinner she refused a drink. She had not had wine with the meal. He caught himself before he chided her for lighting a cigarette. It was like a tap left running during a flood. How in God's name could he bring it up?

"We had a meeting of the Ethics Board today."

"Oh, you hate that."

"Usually, yes. Today was somewhat different. I hate generalities, but today Lodge introduced a specific problem. One of his patients. Anonymously, of course."

She nodded, expelling smoke in a luxurious cloud.

"He has a woman patient whose reaction to a diagnosis raises questions. That was his point."

"Why hasn't he married?"

"Lodge? He's been married twice."

"Twice!" She pulled her knees up on her cushion and turned toward him, bright with interest. She had always been an actress, but this was a masterful performance.

"Neither worked out."

"I suppose it's seeing so many women. I mean treating them."

"He's a very good doctor."

"Not that it can be very sexy. Everyone complaining about this and that."

"Many of his patients are seriously ill."

"Does he go with anyone now?"

"The case he put before us was of a woman who suddenly developed cancer."

"How awful."

"It's not that Lodge blames himself. There are types you can only be sure of after they've happened, and there is almost never time for control, let alone prevention."

"Why should he blame himself?"

"It may make no sense, but doctors sometimes do." He had never spoken to her of his own practice either, not the details. Her interest lay more in the income and the style of life it provided. He wasn't sure she had a very clear notion of the kind of surgery he performed and in which he excelled. He brushed aside the slight annoyance he felt at her disinterest in his work. This conversation was about her, not him—at least that was its aim. Yolande proved remarkably adept at steering away from the relevance to herself of what they were talking about.

"I talked with Lodge privately afterward."

"We have to fix him up with someone."

"I asked him the name of his patient, and he said he wished I hadn't asked."

He fell silent, looking at her, his expression inviting her to confide in him, to spare him the pain of asking her point blank. She let some moments go by before she noticed the silence.

"So?"

"Yolande, you can't just ignore it. It won't go away."

"What are you talking about?"

"If you don't want to go to a stranger for a second opinion, I can get the lab reports and go over the data. I'm sure Lodge is right, but you would feel better, I would feel better, if everything was double checked."

"I don't know what you're talking about."

"I am talking about your appointment with Lodge last week."

"But I didn't have an appointment with him last week."

"Yolande, he as much as told me . . ."

"Told you what?"

Her expression of total incomprehension was too convincing to be feigned. She sat looking at him with parted lips, wary, as if he were mad.

"Max, if you are accusing me of something, just say it."

"You weren't in to see Lodge?"

"No!"

"And you're not ill? You're all right?"

For answer she sat back and opened her arms, as if to exhibit how healthy she was. Looking at his wife's plush inviting body, convinced that beneath that rubescent flesh no civil war of the cells was going on, her days numbered, he took her roughly into his arms and crushed her to him, crying out with relief.

"For God's sake, Max, what's the matter?"

He was literally weeping with joy. "I thought Lodge . . . He as much as said . . . Oh, what a fool I was to leap . . ."

And he crushed her more tightly against him, her great breasts withstanding the pressure and inciting him to increase it. His lips moved to her shoulder, and her fingers moved through his hair. So intense was his desire that it was consummated there on the couch, each of them still half dressed, an impetuous passionate coupling of a kind that had characterized their first months of marriage and then subsided.

Afterward, she said she would have a drink now, and he mixed a brandy Alexander for her. She liked sweet powerful drinks. Then he went upstairs and showered. Standing under the stinging water, he realized that if Yolande was not the patient Lodge had spoken of, someone else was. His relief and joy were tempered by the fact that Lodge had said he knew the woman, and that he would prefer not to reveal her name.

He told himself that it had not been irrational for him to assume that Lodge was trying to tell him about his own wife. Although, in calm retrospect, it was obvious that would have been an extraordinary way to convey such news to an interested party, let alone to a fellow physician. So swiftly had he come to think Lodge meant Yolande that he had forgotten the way he had put it and concentrated on the presumed fact. Who was Lodge referring to?

What woman he knew would turn away from any help and set her face resolutely toward death? Yolande might have done that in a childish unwillingness to face the truth, but Lodge did not seem to have that kind of resistance in mind.

Yolande was surprised when he came downstairs fully dressed.

"Was that just a quickie, doctor?"

He bent to kiss her. "An installment on things to come."

"Aren't you a tiger?"

"Well, I'm not lion."

"Oh." She made a face. "That's awful."

"I have to run by the hospital."

"Stay away from patients you think have terminal cancer."

"At the moment, they'd be safe from me."

"If I'm asleep when you come back, don't wake me."

"How will I know?"

"Ask."

His step was buoyant all the way to his car, but once he got behind the wheel his mind was on the reason for this excursion. He picked up his phone, closed his eyes for a moment and then dialed a number.

"Lodge. You're in."

"Is that you, Max? What is it?"

"I've been thinking of that case you put before us today."

"I wonder if it was wise to do so. I mean in such detail."

"Unless you have an apartment full of naked dancing girls, I'd like to stop by."

"Wouldn't you if I did?"

"I never answer hypothetical questions."

Lodge's apartment looked more like an office than a bachelor's den. His dedication to his calling was everywhere evident—medical journals strewn about, catalogues, advertisements, shelves of videos detailing new procedures. The living room had been turned into a study where Lodge apparently spent most of his time in a chair that was placed between a conventional desk and a computer table, permitting him to swivel from one to the other.

"Let me guess now. What do you do for a living?"

"It's a mess, but it's my mess. It's why I was never a good husband."

He did have some very good scotch, however. He made them both weak drinks and then sat back. "You said you wanted to talk about my case."

"Promise not to laugh, but do you know who I thought you meant?"

"Who?"

"Yolande."

"My God, you didn't. Max, I would have told you, of course, and for many different reasons. Did you say something to her?"

"I have had a very interesting evening."

"Did she throw you out?"

"Nothing so dramatic. You know Yolande."

"She is one of the healthiest patients I have."

"Foolish as I feel, and felt, I came to ask who the woman is. You said I knew her."

"You do."

"Tell me."

He ran the edge of his glass along his lower lip. "I'll do it professionally. Appealing to you as a fellow physician for whatever help you can be."

"How ethical we've all become."

"How prudent, you mean. As in a piece of the rock."

"Who is she?"

"Lucy Flood."

"No!"

Lodge nodded. "I was as surprised as you are. There was the melanoma, as I mentioned, but that seemed completely taken care of. Even so, I was keeping a close watch on her. Not close enough, as it happens. It had been three months since I had seen her. Routine tests produced horrendous results. In that short a time it had spread through her body, everywhere. There are some centers of concentration, but it could never be removed in any significant amount. Still, some surgery could help. Chemotherapy would at least slow it down."

"Giving her what?"

"In time?" He displayed his hands, then picked up his drink again. "She'll never see Christmas."

"And with surgery and chemotherapy?"

"Maybe she'd see Christmas."

"But in what kind of shape?"

"Bald as an egg and sewn up like a baseball, but alive."

"Did you put it this way to her?"

"Of course not."

"But she got the picture."

"I believe in being frank."

Max rattled his glass and then drained it. "Her decision doesn't sound all that hard to understand."

"Now that I've told you, let me ask a favor. For me certainly—this really bothers me; Lucy is a friend as well as a patient—but for her too. Talk to her."

"Talk to her? What can I say that you haven't already said?"

"You talked to Yolande when you thought it was her. What did you say to her?"

It was a telling point, but Max was loath to interfere in Lucy's decision. Now that he knew who it was, he found it hard to imagine that Lucy didn't understand what she was deciding. What would he himself do in the circumstances? He had been in medicine long enough to be wary of going under the knife. Like most surgeons he avoided surgery at all costs. He knew too much to regard any procedure as purely routine.

"I should tell you that I don't think she intends to wait for death to come to her."

"Suicide?"

Lodge nodded. "That's only a guess, but I would wager much on it. It seemed to underlie her resistance to anything that might ameliorate her condition or delay its outcome. She behaved like a woman who didn't intend to wait around for a horrible and painful end. If she wouldn't undergo the procedures, why should she undergo that?"

"Does she know how messy suicide usually is?"

"We never got into that."

"And she never suggested you do a Kevorkian?"

"I hope she knows me better than that. Will you talk to her?"

With his whole being he wanted to say *no, let her be, it's her decision,* but he agreed, first with a gesture, then with a vocal *Yes.* To his surprise and annoyance, Lodge pushed the phone toward him.

"Now?"

"There isn't a lot of time left."

Twenty

Lucy had accepted Warren's offer to take Lorenzo's letter and the envelope containing money to the Federal Express office because she was irked by his suggestion that it would have been a high crime and misdemeanor to use the forms and envelopes that represented the firm's account. Besides, it was a relief to have him out of the house and to be alone. When he called from his office, asking if she minded his catching up on some things there, she had no objection. Why should she? Of course he would sneak away to be with Yolande. If she were really spiteful, she might phone Yolande and just chat a bit, to let them know she was not a complete fool. That was something they would learn in good time anyway. Besides, the prospect of the whole evening to herself was delicious.

She put on all of Mozart's sonatas, placing the CD disks carefully in the player, wanting to hear them in chronological order. She opened a bottle of the Portuguese wine she loved, and from the freezer took the pack of cigarettes she had put there while she was quitting. The idea had been that it would be because she willed it rather than because they were un-available that she no longer smoked cigarettes. With Mozart and wine, she trusted that the old pleasure of smoking would return as it had not when she accepted a cigarette from Alma.

Thus she settled down for a sybaritic evening, alone, ex-isting in the moment, forgetful of the past and above all ignoring the present. What was life but a series of moments?

When the phone rang, her first thought was that Warren had changed his mind, but he would not call to tell her that. It would only mean that Yolande had not been free after all. She picked up the phone and was pleasantly surprised to find it was Max Kramer.

"I want to talk with you."

"So talk."

"Face to face."

"Sounds serious." A vague intimation of trouble came but then went when she recalled Lodge's promise of confidentiality.

"Is Warren there?"

"If he's the one you want to talk with, you could catch him at his office."

"Now?"

She thought of Yolande. "Are you at home?"

He laughed. "But I'm a doctor. Can I stop by?"

"Of course."

After she hung up, she stood and looked at herself in the mirror. She was wearing a silk lounge suit, one of those purchases that is so irresistible when bought and so seldom worn. She put a hand to her hair, turned her face slightly. She had not yet opened the cigarettes and now took the package back to the freezer. She did not want to have a tiresome conversation about smoking, not now. After all, she had quit when it made sense not to smoke, but what point was there now in forgoing its minor pleasure?

She realized that she was expectant, almost excited, that Max was coming. When the four of them had dinner together at the club, particularly on the last occasion, Lucy had thought of herself and Max as old folks, with Warren and Yolande of a younger generation. And it was true, in terms of maturity. Max never spoke of his work unless she asked him, and if he responded, Yolande always cut him off.

"Oh Max, not that. Nobody cares about that. Not when we're trying to enjoy ourselves."

Lucy felt a twinge of resentment and jealousy at Yolande's undoubted good health. Anticipating Max's coming, not wishing to regard her half-conscious fantasy as a matter of quid pro quo, she should resent this interruption of her evening alone but found herself looking forward to talking with Max. They so seldom got a chance really to talk. And this, she realized, would be a final opportunity.

Thoughts about tomorrow were precisely what she did not want to entertain. The fleeting memory of Alma's absurd promise tugged at her heart, and she felt a rush of hope. If only it were so! But she forced such foolishness away. Better to squeeze from her remaining hours what pleasure she could. The die was cast. *Die.* What a word in such a case. If she had life to live she thought she might devote it to the quirks and twists of the language.

"Mozart," Max murmured when she let him in.

"I am indulging myself."

But he had stopped and with closed eyes gave himself up to the strains of Sonata 21. Obviously she had not gotten them into their proper order. This was a particular favorite of hers, but she assumed that, like Bach's Air for G String, it was everyone's favorite. After a moment he opened his eyes.

"Beautiful."

He might have been commenting on her. She took delight in the ambiguity. "I am also drinking wine. A red from Portugal I love. Would you like some?"

"Everywhere I go tonight I am offered alcohol."

"Where have you been?"

"To Lodge's."

Lucy's smile froze. "He couldn't have offered you anything as good as this."

She poured a glass and handed it to him. They had moved into the living room. He looked around. This was her room, the whole house was hers, in the sense of reflecting her tastes, being what she had wanted. Warren was content with whatever she chose, so she had pleased herself.

"Have I ever told you how much I like this room?"

She almost said she would miss it. His mention of Lodge was another warning. Suddenly she was certain why he was here. Wherever such certainties come from, once they arrive there is no disputing them. He knew what Lodge had told her. He was here to plead the case that Lodge had pleaded. If she was not angry it was because it was all too late now. She could listen to whatever he had to say because it could no longer change what would happen on the following day.

"And why are you making the rounds to be offered drinks?" she said, when he was seated in a chair at right angles to the couch on which she sat.

"I think you know."

"Tell me."

"In an ethics meeting at the hospital today, Lodge proposed a problem of a patient who, hearing that she has terminal cancer, refused any treatment that would alleviate or slow the progress of her condition."

"As well as a second opinion."

"Yes."

"But I am going to get one anyway?"

He was visibly relieved that she did not choose to deny she was the woman to whom Lodge referred. It was unpleasant to be treated as a problem in medical ethics.

"So Lodge told you who the patient was?"

"Not by name, no. He was very cagey and then, on the way

148

home, I thought I knew why. I thought he was speaking of Yolande."

"Yolande!"

"She is also a patient of his. He said I knew who the woman was and later that he wished I wouldn't ask her name. I thought he was being subtle."

"But what did you do?"

He smiled ruefully. "We had a scene something like this."

"You told her you thought she was Lodge's hopeless patient?"

"You can imagine how relieved . . ." He stopped, as if pleasure in Yolande's health was somehow an insult to her. He tasted the wine, put down the glass. "What do you plan to do?"

"Accept what surgery and chemotherapy could only postpone."

"Just wait to die?"

"Unless there's a miracle. I'm told I can expect one."

"Lodge gave you hope?"

"Oh no. A friend of mine, a woman who also volunteers at the prison and has a great devotion to Our Lady of Fatima. Do you know of her?"

"Your friend?"

"Her friend. The Blessed Virgin Mary. She talks like that. She used to be a nun. She has promised to pray for me, and she assures me such a prayer will be answered."

"I hope she's right."

"But you think it's all nonsense."

"My opinion on such matters is worthless."

"Without a miracle, I know what to expect."

"I wonder if you do."

"Death."

His manner now was that of the physician. How often had

he gone through this with patients of his own? She wondered, do they keep score, balancing the successes against the failures? Max was accounted one of the best surgeons in the area, doubtless because his survival rate was far greater than his losses. Did the fact that ultimately all patients are lost ever affect the desire to go on?

"Lucy, have you ever seen anyone die?"

"No."

"Sometimes it happens without those in the room even noticing what has happened. At other times, the moment itself is horrible, a great thrashing physical struggle that is finally over."

"How will it be for me?"

"The moment itself? Peaceful I should say. In your case, it is what leads up to it that can be more or less bad."

"But always bad?"

"The pain can be controlled. We're less reluctant now to give adequate doses. In the past we acted as if we were afraid of making addicts of the dying."

"You're more vivid than Lodge was."

"He is still stunned that this should have occurred. Naturally he blames himself, though without any basis. This came about so suddenly . . . I am of course quoting him. He told you all this?"

"Yes."

"You are very philosophical about it. That's good. Lodge thought that you were deciding at a time when you weren't yourself, in a state of shock. You haven't changed your mind?"

"No."

"Nothing that I've said changes your mind?"

"The choice isn't attractive. Submit myself to some dubious procedures with awful side effects but no sure effect on the progress of the disease, or to leave bad enough alone. Either way I die. I suppose neither way is very dignified."

"Lodge thought that perhaps a third alternative had occurred to you."

"He gave me none." She strove to retain her La dame des camellias tranquility.

"Of course he wouldn't. He worries that you might think of taking your own life."

"Suicide?"

"Have you thought of killing yourself?"

She leaned toward him, putting her hand on his. "I haven't the courage to kill myself."

He turned his hand and clasped hers. She had told him what he had come to hear.

"Have you told Warren?"

"No."

She looked him directly in the eye. He understood. What she had felt when they had all dined together had been true. She and Max understood one another, he knew what she thought of Warren, she knew what he thought of Yolande. Here they were on the eve of her death, caught up in the most solemn of conversations, in a room that was conducive to pensive matters. The intricacies of Mozart continued to make sense of the passage of time. She tugged on his hand and, like a dancer he rose from his chair, ducked under their held hands and sat beside her. She lifted her face to his.

Twenty-one

Unable to get through, Crowe put off sleep until they answered the phone. Just when he was convinced that the girl had talked Larry into bailing out—a thought that should have been welcome, but felt like a betrayal—he tried once more. Bingo.

"We were out," she said.

"Celebrating?"

"That's tomorrow night, isn't it?"

"We hope."

"Is anything wrong?"

"Only that I've gotten myself mixed up with a couple of goddam kids."

"I think you want to talk to Larry."

"I think I may just call the whole thing off."

Away from the phone she called to Larry, twice, the second one a scream, and then, to the accompaniment of a flushing toilet, he came on.

"Larry here."

"Here sounds like the bathroom."

"Mad says you been trying to reach us."

"Imagine that. You do remember what's coming up tomorrow, don't you?"

"You're kidding."

"I never kid. I think I'm cutting you out of the deal."

"You can't do that!"

"I just did. Your whole damned attitude is wrong. I don't know what Lorenzo was thinking of when he recommended you look me up. This isn't your trade."

"It is. It is. Let me show you."

"You're liable to get all of us in trouble. Does a fighter go out on the town before a big match? Does he have his girl-friend with him? You're not serious."

"Hey, we went out to eat."

"How many beers you have?"

"None. No drink at all. We were in a fast food place. I had a Diet Coke."

"From the beginning, everything told against you."

"In the beginning you damn near killed me."

"I must have jarred your brains."

A long pause. He could hear the kid breathing. Then, "You know what's wrong with this call, Crowe?"

"What?"

"You're making it. If you planned to cut and run, you'd just do it. You wouldn't call up and preach sermons to me."

"I figured I owed it to Lorenzo."

"You'd just be outta here. I'd show up tomorrow and no you. That's what you'd do."

It was Crowe's turn to say nothing for a while. He didn't like this kid telling him what he would or wouldn't do. He sounded like a shrink. They liked to ask a few questions and then talk about you as if you were a watch that didn't run too well but could be fixed.

"You're right."

"I am?" He laughed. "I was just talking."

"I know."

"So we're on."

"You're on."

"Huron. That's one of the great lakes. Know how to remember them? HOMES."

He rattled them off. Crowe closed his eyes and shook his head. The kid made it easier all the time. Thinking about Lorenzo made him hesitate to do this, but the kid was worse than he thought. No one would willingly work with him. Crowe felt he was doing all sorts of people he would never know and who would never work with Larry a big favor.

"You must have been great in school."

"Hey, grades aren't everything."

He laid it out for him then. Be at the fountain of the mall at eleven the next morning. He would tell him in detail then how it would go.

"The way we've been over it?"

"No. That was to teach you things. Never tell anybody how you're going to do a job before you do it. What I've told you till now is inoperative."

"Madeline wants to talk to you."

"Phil?"

She had never called him Phil before. No one called him Phil. He smiled at the receiver. What did she want?

"Sounds like you been thinking of calling it off."

"Larry will tell you what I said."

"I've been listening in, but I couldn't follow all that well. You don't have to worry about our celebrating tonight."

That got to him. What brass, apologizing to him for the kid with him right there, as much as saying she knew Larry was a joke. She was lucky he was. Any other guy would give her a belt. But the kid had used her as a whore from the word go, putting her on to him even after Crowe walloped him with the butt of his gun. You can't trust a guy who treats a girl that way. Not that she was much better. She had to go along with it, and the only reason a broad did that was as a favor to the guy that put her up to it. He gave up. He didn't understand either one of them, and he was through trying.

"Maybe Larry should drop out."

A struggle and then Larry had the phone. "I'll be there at eleven tomorrow morning."

Twenty-two

Max left before Warren returned. Lucy remained in the living room as if to review what had happened and savor it all again. There were the wine glasses, Mozart still played, but she did not know what she felt. It did not occur to her to clean up the room before Warren returned.

"Two glasses?"

"Max was here."

"Max."

"He dropped by, and I offered him some of the wine I was drinking."

A merely factual statement. She was not explaining, certainly not apologizing. Warren had betrayed her first. No, she did not feel avenged either. What had happened with Max had happened, like an earthquake or tropical storm. There had been an awesome inevitability in their making love, as if they had been tacitly planning it for years, something for the grown-ups when Warren and Yolande were not there. She might have asked Warren if he had been with Yolande, but she dismissed the thought that there was any similarity at all between his silly affair with Yolande and the tornado that had swept Max and herself into its vortex.

"What did he want?"

"He expected to find you here."

"What did you tell him?"

"What you told me."

"Don't you believe me?"

"Of course I believe you."

He wanted her to call him a liar, to accuse him, to provide him with an occasion to be a repentant spouse, come back to ask that all be forgiven. She felt no anger or resentment. He simply wasn't worthy of it. The thought that she had ennobled Warren and Yolande by making arrangements with Crowe in such a way that the two of them would come under suspicion after she was dead suddenly angered her. Had she really thought it mattered that he was unfaithful to her?

Warren picked up the glasses and started for the kitchen with them, as if he were destroying evidence for a client. Lucy was sure that his imagination could not accommodate the thought of her being unfaithful to him. But it was pity rather than contempt she felt. This was the man she had married, till death did them part. Well, let the break be clean.

She decided to delay Crowe if only to make clear that Warren and Yolande had nothing to do with her decision. Clear to whom? It is impossible to live life without the thought of a recording angel taking it all down, the simple honest account for the archives of the universe.

"Did you mail my letter?"

He came out of the kitchen. "How can you listen to that god-awful music?"

"Warren, that is Mozart."

"That's what I mean. Put on some music a person can listen to."

"You choose something."

"I'm going to bed."

"I think I'll sit up for awhile."

"I don't know how you can listen to that stuff."

"It's a flaw in my character. Did you mail the letter?"

"No. I sent it Federal Express."

"Thank you."

"You're welcome."

This polite exchange might have been a trading of insults.

"I'm going up."

"Good night. Thanks for mailing the letter, Warren."

He marched upstairs without another word.

The thought of her sitting up down there without him, self-contained in her solitude, thoughtful with wine and music, elusive, got to Warren. The offhand way she had mentioned Max's visit angered him. What in hell had that been about? Warren could not believe that Lucy had been unfaithful to him. It would be futile for him even to try to think of her in the role of the cheating wife. A wife like Yolande. He shook his head. Impossible.

In bed, he could not sleep. Maybe he could trust Lucy, but what about Max? A man doesn't drop by to visit a beautiful woman when her husband is not at home just to pass the time of day. Particularly at night. The sonofabitch. Warren no longer felt even a tinge of regret for having arranged for Max to be removed from Yolande's life. That was a little treat in store for the two of them. After all, at first Phelps thought it was Yolande making arrangements for Lucy to be shot. Warren had found that oddly plausible even when he knew it wasn't true. It made sense that Yolande might think, with Lucy out of the way, that . . . Well, think what?

Lucy had hired a killer to get rid of him. Don't forget that, he instructed himself. He sat up and threw back the covers. He had been too smart for her, but she didn't know that yet. Had she and Max met tonight to anticipate the freedom tomorrow was supposed to bring? Warren smiled grimly. Max would have been behind it all, of course; it was the only way

Lucy could tolerate his advances, if she were no longer encumbered with a husband. The bastard. Max deserved what he was going to get, no doubt of that. And so did Lucy.

He liked the second thought less than the first. It suggested that Lucy preferred Max to him. Max? He was so immersed in his practice he didn't even know that his wife was crawling the walls. That seemed to rule out any romantic designs on Lucy. Max must have checked out of the sex department, too tired and busy even to need it anymore. The poor ass. Warren felt he was punishing the surgeon for his absence of humanity, the common touch, some sense of what a woman expected of a man. Did he dream that with Lucy he could make a comeback?

He went to the head of the stairs and listened. That goddam music was still on, the volume turned down somewhat, but still booping away. Warren was convinced that people only pretended to like that kind of stuff; it was a restless agitation of sound without any real tune or rhythm as far as he could see. It must be like exercise, painful, but you went on with it because it was supposed to be good for you.

As he passed the door of his den, the glow of the light on the power surge protector caught his eye. He went inside and closed the door before turning on the light. There was a dedicated telephone line on his fax machine. He picked up the phone and was about to dial when it occurred to him to press redial. The number that beeped out was Yolande's, the very number he had been about to call, the last number he had dialed on the fax phone was hers. Good God, if Lucy had ever really suspected him of hanky-panky he had left clues all over the place. Just press redial and she would hear, as he now did, the phone ringing in Yolande's bedroom.

Ringing but not being answered. He was about to hang up when the answering machine was activated.

"Hi. This is Yolande. I can't come to the phone just now. Please leave a message at the beep and don't forget to mention the date and time. Max won't get me a machine that records those, the old cheapskate."

Warren did not record anything at the beep. He pressed down on the receiver, then released it, and punched redial again. He let the phone ring through to the answering machine and then slammed it down. His mind filled with the thought of Yolande in bed with Max. "Don't answer it," she would say in the whisper he knew so well. "Let it ring."

He was infuriated by the thought that Max, after prowling around Lucy for half the night, had gone home and jumped into the sack with Yolande. None of this matched his thoughts of a few minutes before, but Warren was beyond the hobgoblin of consistency. Max had become the enemy, a threat from every quarter. Tomorrow, the day of reckoning, could not come too soon.

In the morning he called Yolande on the way to his office.

"Max still there?"

"Is that you, Warren?"

"Yes."

"Was it you who phoned last night?"

"What time?"

"It was you!"

"I hope I disturbed something."

"You did." She paused and his tortured thoughts began. "My sleep."

"Yeah."

"I took two sleeping pills and went out like a light, but the phone pulled me almost awake and then my sleep was restless most of the night."

"Max was here last night."

"Here?"

"He dropped in to see Lucy."

"That's nonsense. He and Lodge got together about some problem at the hospital."

"He was here. Drinking with Lucy."

"Well, that must have been some orgy, those two."

"Don't underestimate your husband."

"I was thinking of your wife."

"It must run in the family."

"Warren, I am beginning to worry about you. What you told me the other day? I have given it serious thought and I think you must be losing your mind. I even thought I was losing mine. You did tell me that Lucy had hired someone to kill you, didn't you?"

"That was a joke."

"A joke!"

"Well, a test. I wanted to know how you would react."

"I felt like killing you myself."

Carrying on this conversation, negotiating traffic, on edge because of a restless night, he wondered what he would do if he were free, free of everything—free of Lucy, free of Yolande, starting off with a blank slate.

Max's visit, their incredible coupling that somehow was not macabre, a frolic in the cemetery, and then silly Warren pouting and demanding an explanation, washed Lucy's mind free of the certitude that had been guiding her since the fateful appointment with Lodge. Had she actually arranged for her own killing?

The whole sequence, the first conversations with Lorenzo, then contacting Crowe and the elaborate ritual dance before he would admit that he was the man she sought, the planning and subterfuge to prevent him from learning that she herself was his intended victim—the whole sequence, and each part in it, was so far removed from what had hitherto been reality that it seemed to her now that she had moved from step to step without really believing that such things could be true.

Now with a clarity of mind brought on by something even more incredible, permitting Max to make love to her, surrendering to him right here in the living room of her home with her favorite music an ironic measure of their frantic lovemaking, she realized something. When passion had run its course, they had subsided into the ordered emotions of Mozart's music and the brief excursion from reason came into perspective.

She did not want to die.

As long as she was alive, and feeling as well as she ever had, it was an obscenity to brood about death, to run to meet it. The diagnosis was no more real than the arrangements she had made with Crowe or what she and Max had done together. The whole of reality was beyond belief, not just hired assassins and adulterous lovers, but the supposed routine and ordinary as well. Nothing was ordinary. Birth and death and everything in between were miracles of unlikelihood.

She had to stop what she had begun. Crowe could keep the money; he should be pleased to be paid without having to add to the weight of his sins. *Sins*. She felt that Alma was occupying some back bench in her mind, introducing a vocabulary and criteria of appraisal, absurdly familiar commonplaces that no one believed anymore. What she had arranged was a far greater sin, bringing about her own death. Would Crowe the killer flinch at the thought of killing himself? Of course he would.

She had been moving around the living room collecting glasses, straightening up, letting the music continue. How could she stop Crowe? By failing to show up as agreed. It was that simple, was it not? Unless his method was to settle on one time and place and then reintroduce the element of surprise. He must always be on the alert to the chance that he was being set up.

Lucy stopped, arrested by her reflection in the mirror over the fireplace. *I am beautiful,* she thought, a factual observation, no quiver of pleasure. It was perfectly possible that Crowe had imagined that all these telephone conversations, the elaborate plans obliquely made, were part of a scheme to entrap him. Warren was known at Michigan City, after all, and not as a friend of the inhabitants. Several of them were there because of his efforts. Any alumnus of the prison would have to suspect that the wife of a criminal lawyer was a decoy when she began to make arrangements to have someone killed.

Even if the someone was herself.

She had tried to conceal that from Crowe, pretending to be Yolande. He had been equally deceptive and misleading, and what had seemed merely the circumspection of his craft now suggested that he had suspected her all along. He might be planning revenge rather than the fulfillment of a business agreement.

He could be watching this house now. She could already be under surveillance. This might be her final hour.

She began to turn off the lights, moving in a swift crouch from lamp to lamp, feeling like a fool, but filled with a fear that had been absent for weeks. Fear of death.

She crept upstairs to her bed and did not sleep. Throughout the night, she was aware of an equally restless Warren in the bed next to hers.

Twenty-three

Crowe got to the mall early, anxious for the girl and Larry to show up, and suddenly the kid was there, five minutes late, but for him that wasn't bad. The girl was with him, her hair skinned back and done up in a ponytail. She looked about twelve years old. Larry looked the way he would in a line-up if he weren't stopped right now from going into the life. He would be in and out of the work in the same day. Crowe strolled to the escalator, and as he was descending, Madeline looked up and saw him. She tugged at Larry's sleeve, and they were at the bottom to meet him.

"Stay behind me," he said.

He threaded his way through the shoppers to a fast food franchise where he took a table. First Larry and then the girl sat across from him. Larry looked around.

"Hey, this is like the one at the oasis."

"What oasis?"

Beneath the table Crowe's ankle was kicked. She must have meant it for Larry.

"We took the toll road down," he said, hunching forward. "So what's the plan?"

He would have accepted Larry's explanation if she hadn't kicked. Obviously she thought he was nuts for mentioning it. Why should he care if they stopped at an oasis on their way down? Something was going on. He told himself again that he could abort the whole thing, forget the money, get the hell away from these two. It was like remembering an old song. They had been trouble from the beginning and the only reason he had stuck with the contract was the girl. Look at her. There wasn't enough meat on her to squeeze, she probably jumped into the sack with anything that moved, and he was panting after her like a kid himself. But now that was a reason for going ahead, not backing off.

"You've studied the photographs."

"Yup."

"You'd know her anywhere?"

"Yes."

"I hope you're not counting on me to identify her, because you are going to be on your own. You want to get into the business? Okay. This is going to be your chance. You're going to do this solo, and you're going to come through, right?"

"Where you going to be?"

"You worry about things like that and you're going to bungle it. In your mind you have to think this is your job, there's only you, you can't depend on anyone else."

Larry nodded and looked serious.

"You got the stun gun."

"My bow and arrow? I got it."

"Okay. You'll be stationed on the upper level, overlooking the fountain. Your shot will be down and away. If you need two, it'll be no problem. Chances are no one will see the line of fire. You can walk away from it. Do that in any case. Don't run. Don't call attention to yourself. Get rid of the weapon."

"Get rid of it."

"You won't have time to break it down and conceal it. Find the place you'll stash it beforehand."

Madeline said, "When will she be here?"

Unnecessarily, he looked at his watch. "Three o'clock."

"That's hours from now."

"Look at it from her point of view."

"I don't want to think of it." She shuddered. It was when she looked fragile and defenseless that he liked her most. "Where will you be?"

"You'll be with me."

He waited for a protest but none came. Again he thought of the oasis. Were they plotting against him as he was plotting against Larry? He could already see Larry in the can, hair cut, wearing denims and shoes that weighed ten pounds. It would be the making of him. Maybe he could be assigned to his uncle's cell.

"How does he get paid?" she asked.

"It's about time that came up. I already have the money."

Larry smiled with half his mouth. "You've got the money?"

"Yes."

"All of it?"

"I don't work any other way."

"But what's to stop you from just taking off?"

"I'm a pro."

Larry glanced at Madeline. There was some secret they had.

Crowe said, "We meet in Birmingham, that's in Alabama, at the airport, on Wednesday. Get there as quickly as you can, though. It's a good place not to get caught."

"Why Birmingham?"

"In honor of Martin Luther King."

Larry looked blank. Hadn't he heard of King?

"Ask Lorenzo to explain it."

Larry asked her what Crowe had meant, and Madeline

told him it was a joke.

"I don't get it."

"You will."

"Yeah."

"Larry, have you ever really looked at his eyes?"

"Every time I talk with him."

"Ha. You're always running to catch up whenever he talks to you."

He hit her. A wide sweep of his arm and then his open hand slapping against her face, sending her stumbling. She ended up on her butt, and people paused and stopped and stared at Larry and then at her. It wasn't just the embarrassment Madeline felt, or the pain, but the emptiness that he would treat her like that. Her old man had hit her mother whenever he was drunk, and Madeline had sworn to herself that she would never let a man do that to her. She had planned to kill her father some day for doing that to her mother, and she would do the same to any man who hit her.

Larry came toward her, his face going from angry through half a dozen other looks.

"Geez, Mad."

He reached out a hand, but she turned away and got to her feet. She headed for the escalator and rode it down to the main level of the mall. Behind her, Larry kept calling out her name, getting excited again. To hell with him. To hell with him and Crowe and this whole crazy business. She had the five thousand dollars and she was leaving.

She was six feet from the public phone when she realized it was ringing. A couple kids wearing baseball caps and huge unlaced tennis shoes pumped full of air stopped and gawked at the phone. Then one of them reached out and picked it up.

"Hey," he said.

His mouth never closed as he listened, looking at the other

167

guy whose baseball cap read Sox as if he could hear what he was hearing. A stupid wondering smile twisted his rubber lips.

"Where?" He took the phone from his mouth and asked, "Where is this?"

"Where's what?"

"Where's this phone?"

"In your frigging hand," Sox said. "What kind of question is that?"

Sox got the phone rammed at him in answer. He took it and struck a pose. "Yeees?" He listened, eyes closed, a supercilious smile on his face. "Why this here's the mall, ma'am. The University Park Mall." He took the phone from his ear, stared at it, then tossed it to rubber lips.

"She hung up."

Rubber lips didn't. He let the phone swing free on its metal cable and sauntered away with his friends. Madeline picked up the dangling phone and put it to her ear. There was only a buzzing sound. She returned it to its hook.

She was sure it was the same woman who had called this number before, the woman who had a contract with Crowe. She wasn't supposed to get in touch with Crowe. The wheels had begun their final turn. Something was wrong. On the upper level, Larry was still calling her name, but she seemed to be the only one in the mall who could hear him. He gestured with his arm, the one with which he had hit her.

"C'mon." He hunched his shoulder. "Bring it."

He meant her bag. He meant the money. She lifted her hand and gave him the finger.

Warren called again and his whining, accusing tone grated on her.

"I did call you last night."

"I was home."

"Was Max?"

She just looked at the phone, saying nothing.

"Did he come home to you after he left Lucy?"

"Warren, we have been through this. I know Max, so don't try to tell me things about him I know could not have happened. And I know you too. Are you jealous of Max?"

"I've got no reason to be."

"That's what I said."

"I meant something else."

She made an impatient sound, then audibly took in air. "Do I have to remind you that your wife made arrangements with someone to have you killed?"

"I thought you didn't believe that."

"You do."

"I've taken care of that."

"Have you?"

"Yes."

"What exactly does that mean?"

"You'll see."

"Where are you calling from?"

"My car."

"Are you being followed?"

She hung up without waiting for his answer and went into the bathroom, closing the door and running water in the sink to drown out the sound of the ringing phone.

Later when she came out and picked up the phone she half expected to find Warren still on the line.

She found Phelps in the Yellow Pages under private investigators. He recognized her voice, he said, which was eerie.

"Warren says he has taken care of matters."

"Did he say what he meant?"

"What could he mean?"

"Lots of things. And nothing."

"He's talked to that man. You know the one I mean."

"How do you plan to spend the day, Mrs. Kramer?"

"Why?"

"It might be a good idea to be especially careful."

She was infuriated, as she had been at Warren on the veranda of the club. It was bad enough then, but now this private detective was trying to frighten her. She told him to just mind his own business.

"That's what I'm doing. Thanks for the call."

The police were in on it now, but so far they were taking their cue from Phelps, probably not eager to stick their necks out too far just on his say-so. They studied the photographs, they watched the film, they saw the transcript of the exchange between the kid and Warren and decided to be noncomittally cooperative. Fair enough.

"Which one's your client?" Molson, a detective lieutenant, asked.

"Warren Flood. I'm legally bound to tell you these things."

"He hired you?"

"It's a long story." And one he had already told Molson's superior. Even now, despite all the proof he had, Phelps had difficulty believing his own story. The cops took over surveillance of Crowe and his two accomplices; they would unobtrusively escort Lucy wherever she went, remaining in contact with those watching the assassins. It had passed out of Phelps's hands, but he intended to keep his own eye on Warren. Molson's expression suggested that Phelps was letting his client down, but that he approved of it. Phelps seethed with the conviction that Warren had tried to use him, set him up, betray him, make a goddam fool of him. His reaction drew on the deep well of his resentment at his own blighted law career. Phelps was willing to admit that, at least to himself. Sure, he had often thought that Warren was the partner he might have become. But he had not resented the man, personally; he did not deserve this kind of treatment from a man who was a kind of colleague.

Yolande's call would have told him Warren was in his office even if Phelps didn't know it already. He was back in his van in the parking basement of the garage of the building in which he, like Warren, had his offices. As a grudging courtesy, Molson had agreed to keep Phelps in on the police movements. Phelps had their frequency anyway, and it was soon clear that if he had relied on Molson he would have been almost completely in the dark.

A team identifying themselves as Alpha reported on Crowe and the two kids. Beta had Lucy in sight. Sitting in his van, following their reports, Phelps waited in vain for Molson to let him know these things were going on.

Alpha reported that the trio had split up. The young guy took a swing at the girl and she took off. Where was the young guy now? Catching up with Crowe. Phelps could picture that welterweight hurrying along a step behind Crowe, talking his head off while Crowe ignored him. Alpha was told to stay with the two men. Phelps contacted his own man Simpson at the mall.

"Someone staying with the girl?"

"Agnes."

He called Agnes. Her voice was faint and he told her to speak up.

"Shhh. I'm in the ladies room."

"She with you?"

"Next stall."

"Good work."

He cut back to Simpson. "Stay with Crowe and the kid."

"They split up."

"What?"

They had gone into L. S. Ayers, to the men's department and waded through the racks of ready-to-wear suits and into the dressing rooms in back. The kid had come out immediately, but Crowe was still in there.

"Any cops around?"

"Uh huh."

"Anyone with the kid?"

"I don't know."

"Stick with Crowe."

Crowe had been a damned fool to stay with those two this long. Not only were they making a circus out of the main job, they were double-crossing him with Warren. Had he told the kid to beat it? Clobbering the girl in the mall like that, the kid might have made a public address announcement that they had arrived.

Maybe the kid didn't know that the hit wasn't scheduled for the mall.

Phelps checked with his man Clauson. "What's Dr. Kramer doing?"

"What he's been doing since six this morning. Operating."

Max was accounted for. Lucy was accounted for. Marge was assigned to her. Always put a woman on a woman. When he worked alone, Phelps had lost enough female subjects in powder rooms to have learned the lesson. Marge reported that Lucy was still in the house.

Phelps had the complete picture thanks to his own people. The police called a couple times, feebly corroborating a fraction of what he already knew. Max was in the operating room, doing open-heart surgery. Lucy was still inside the house Warren had left more than an hour ago. This was a Thursday.

The make he had on Lucy told him that one day a month she did volunteer work at Michigan City. On a Thursday. This wasn't that Thursday. If she kept to her pattern, she would have lunch at the country club and from two to five be at the children's hospital. But this was not just another day. If Crowe did his job, this was Lucy's last day. Why had she been trying to reach that public phone at the mall?

Madeline had thought about it first when she went by the lockers and into the Ladies room. She made up her mind inside and got the money out of her bag, wrapped a couple paper towels around it, and then went out to the lockers. It took quarters. In went the package, a twist of the key and then going back into the john she nearly ran into the woman who wore the ankle-length coat over jeans and a sweater.

Back in a stall, Madeline held the locker key in her cupped palm, a five-thousand-dollar key with the number of the locker on it. Lose that and so long money. Her problem was she didn't know what to do. Her anger had cooled and just walking off alone with the money didn't sound like too hot an idea. A woman in the next stall was whispering. Madeline bent over and looked. Only one pair of feet.

Larry was a jerk, but she would miss him. They had hung in there together for weeks. But it wasn't just the money. He was in danger with Crowe and refused to admit it. If she didn't look out for the idiot, who would? Besides, she had to get back at him for slugging her.

If she wore a bra she could have put the key there. She tried her panties, putting it right down in the crotch, but moving around a bit in the locked stall showed she didn't want it there. She took the lace from her gym shoe, strung the key on it and tied it around her neck.

After all that, she decided she better keep the money with

173

her. She was going back for Larry and if she could get him to go they might not have time to make a trip to the locker. Outside in the hall again, she had just got the key in the lock and turned it when someone spoke behind her. She turned. It was Rubber Lips and Sox. Sox held out his hand.

"Lemme have the key, okay? Save me a little money."

The key was still on her shoelace. She put the package under her arm. While she was drawing the key off the lacing, her arm's pressure on the package lessened, and it fell to the floor. The paper towels burst open and money poured out.

Crowe had the silencer attached to his gun, which was in the bag slung over his shoulder. Under its outer flap he had made the opening through which he put his hand. His finger rested on the trigger, his thumb on the safety. He had been armed and ready since arriving at the mall.

Larry came up from behind and fell in step with him. He was alone.

"Where's Madeline?"

"I told her to wait."

Crowe stopped. "For what?"

"For us."

"We're not going back."

"Why not?"

"This isn't the place. I told you. No one knows my plan before it goes into execution."

"Then what the hell you got me practicing for?"

"Practice makes perfect." Crowe had a stock of such phrases, the fruit of a calendar he'd had in the reform school. Each page had the date and phrases that were mint new to Crowe and stuck to his mind like flies to flypaper. Honesty is the best policy. A fool and his money are soon parted.

"Where are we going?"

"Go get her."

"Forget about her. She doesn't want to be part of it. She's always working on me to back out. Let her go. We don't need her."

"Go get her."

Larry's shoulders slumped, and he tried a sheepish smile. "I hit her."

"Yeah."

"Knocked her on her ass. She took off."

Crowe started back the way they had come, eyes straight ahead, mind a blank. He wasn't going to ditch her. He couldn't. She knew too much, and now she had reason to do Larry in. How could she know that Crowe was going to take care of this grinning yo-yo once and for all?

"You're right," Larry said, keeping up. "She's got the money."

"What money?"

"I'll tell you later."

Crowe grabbed him with his free hand and stopped him. When he faced Larry he had the gun on him, a flick of his thumb, a squeeze of this finger, that's all it would take.

"What money?"

"I told you she's been after me to get out of this."

It was all Crowe could do not to pull the trigger. He fixed the kid with his eyes until he had his full attention. "Tell me."

He got it out, but as a tale of Madeline's treachery. They had met with Warren Flood in an oasis on the toll road last night. That's what all the secrecy was about.

"And he gave you some money."

"He gave it to Madeline."

"So you would take out Dr. Kramer?"

Larry snorted. "He couldn't wait to pass over the money."

"And Madeline's got it."

"Yeah."

"How much?"

"I don't know. She counted it. What did I care? I wasn't going to do what he asked."

"Money doesn't interest you?"

"It can't buy me."

He said he had last seen Madeline going down on the escalator. Crowe waved Larry on first and then got on. While they were descending he saw Madeline. She was between two kids wearing baseball caps, and the way they were moving her along her feet hardly touched the ground. Then Larry spotted her too. Crowe nodded. When they were on the main floor, he sent Larry out on the left flank while he took the right. A pincers movement.

Phelps listened as Warren tried to track down Max. Where did the stupid ass think a surgeon would be at this hour of the day? Yolande hung up on him, Max's office tried to make an appointment for Warren with the doctor, finally it was Lucy who told her husband the obvious.

"He's a doctor, Warren."

"Is that why he makes house calls?"

"Oh for heaven's sake."

"Did he come for the big farewell?"

The silence on the line was eloquent, and in two ways. Warren seemed to realize he had said more than he intended; Lucy now knew that her plan was known.

"What are you talking about?"

"I'm just talking. I'm still trying to figure out what is going on in my house when I am not there."

"What did you mean by saying farewell?"

"It's what people say when they leave. He did leave, didn't he?"

"That is good-bye, not farewell. Neither Max nor I would have any occasion to say farewell. Do you understand?"

Warren escaped by saying he had a call on another line. Phelps was driving the van out of the garage before the conversation was over. He was assigning himself to Lucy.

What a goddam mess this was turning into. Phelps could see a significance in Max's calling on Lucy even if Warren couldn't. Doctors don't make house calls, yet Max had, and it provided an explanation for the most vexing aspect of this whole case. At first, it had looked as if Yolande was plotting to get rid of Lucy, but it became inescapable that Lucy was taking out a contract on herself. Why? Her health, improbable as that sounded, could be an explanation. But Warren, consistently stupid, had tried to make Max the target. He had paid money to the two dissolute young people Crowe had allowed to associate with himself, and chances are that, with the money in hand, they would do nothing. If they worked with Crowe, they would play Crowe's game, and he was in town to do Lucy's bidding.

What did she mean when she told Warren that she had no occasion to say farewell? That sounded like she was calling it off. But that couldn't be. Crowe was not behaving like a man whose mission had been aborted.

And then Phelps received the report that the girl was taking off with two young men, and Crowe and Larry were in hot pursuit.

When the package burst open, revealing the money, Madeline dropped to her knees in order to gather it up, but Rubber Lips's huge gym shoe kicked it out of her reach and Sox, grabbing her by the hair, pulled her to her feet. She brought her knee sharply into his groin, and he yelped in pain. For the second time that morning, she was hit in the face. Rubber Lips grabbed her from behind. She struggled to free herself, and the key fell on the floor.

"Six-ty fo-ah," Rubber lips read. He had let go of her as soon as the key hit and gone for it. The money was already stuffed inside his shirt.

Sox hit her again without warning. She tried to kick him in the groin, but he had enough of that. He grabbed her ankle and twisted it, filling her with stabbing pain. Once more she hit the floor, and they were crouched beside her.

"Where'd did you get this money?"

"He'll be here in a minute." As she said it, she could picture Larry hurrying away with Crowe.

Rubber Lips became thoughtful and Sox, holding his crotch, looked down the short corridor to the mall.

"Come on," Rubber Lips said, pulling her up. Pain shot through her when she put weight on her foot.

"What's wrong?"

"I think he broke my ankle."

"Good."

"Take her arm," Rubber Lips said.

"What for? Leave her. Let's get out of here."

"Take her arm, man."

Sox was the Larry of this combo. He did what he was told. Soon she was being half-carried along through the mall, more certain than ever that Larry had written her off and that she was at the mercy of these two morons. Even if she broke free, she wouldn't be able to run. Her ankle throbbed now even though she avoided using her right foot. Let them carry her . . .

"Wait," she cried when they were outside and crossing to where parked cars were forming a growing design on the vast paved surface of the lot. "Wait, for godsake."

They slowed anyway, two faces pushing into hers. In Crowe's eyes she had seen cold malice, but now she was looking into vacant indifference. They would stomp her here in the lot, push her out of a car barrelling down a highway, strangle her—but with no more calculation than they would swat a fly.

"That money," she said.

"What about it?"

They stopped, and she could have cried out with relief until Sox let go of her arm and she had to put pressure on her foot and felt the renewal of stabbing pain. She hobbled to a car and rested against its fender.

"It's no good."

Dumb reaction from Rubber Lips. He rummaged inside his shirt and brought out a one-hundred-dollar bill and stared at it.

"Looks real, doesn't it?"

While they puzzled about this, she babbled on, a story that she was here to deliver this batch to a purchaser, she worked for the engraver, and he and the purchaser were waiting for her, and what good was the money to them? Spend it and they were goners.

"I don't believe her."

"How the hell would you know a good one-hundred-dollar bill?"

"I know she's lying."

Sox would have hit her again, just to hit her, but Rubber Lips stopped him. He was thinking, the effort all over his face.

"Where are these two guys?" He added, as if to himself, "They'll want it back."

"Yeah," Sox agreed. "Where are they?"

And then like the goddam cavalry, angels of mercy, she saw first Crowe and then Larry moving toward them through the parked cars.

"They'd like to meet a couple bright boys like you two."

"Yeah?"

"Someone to sweep up, carry out the garbage, kiss ass, you know."

"Hey!" Rubber Lips brought one fist into her stomach and would have hit her again but something stopped him. A little *phhht,* the dim light in his eyes got dimmer, and blood bubbled from his mouth as he staggered a few steps and then fell. Sox watched all this with his mouth hanging open. Then Larry called out.

"Hey, you black bastard."

Sox turned to face the funny little gun. Larry held it in both hands, raised, and he had on the big grin. Crowe angled in, holding his weapon in one hand.

"He's mine," he said, all business.

"No," Larry shouted.

They were fighting over her. A minute before she was at the mercy of these two monsters, and now Larry and Crowe both wanted to rid her of the second. Crowe must have taken out the Rubber Lips.

Madeline felt a smile forming on her lips as she concentrated on Larry, wondering if he would do what Crowe told him or act like a big boy for a change. Sox was terrified into silence, looking at the two armed men, looking down at his buddy. As if in slow motion, Madeline watched Larry steady his weapon a final time, and then his finger moved. She felt only a slight irritation in her chest before lights began to blaze on, one bank after another, a vast vault full of light and then, abruptly, darkness.

Crowe took out the second one, a clean shot in the chest,

dropping him next to the first, knowing he would fold up the way he did and sink to the pavement. And then the girl slid down the side of the car she'd been leaning against, a half smile frozen on her lips. She hit the pavement and tipped sideways. Larry, still holding the stun gun in both hands, stared at the girl.

"Mad? Mad!" He glanced at Crowe, realizing what he'd done.

Then he was on his knees next to her, lifting her from the pavement, trying to get the lifeless body into his arms. No point in any of that. She was gone.

Crowe refused to believe it. Not Madeline. No!

Pain ripped through him. Crowe realized he had known her only a few days, yet he knew her better than any other woman. She had made a goddam fool of him, more than once, but there had been the other times as well. The gun he held, the one he had used to kill the two blacks, was the one she had lifted from him, leaving him standing in a shower, eager to get to her. In his mind's eye he saw himself slip into the motel bed and talk to her in the dark before he reached out and found she wasn't there.

But there had been other times as well, times unlike he had ever known. He liked her sass, he liked the way he didn't know what she'd say or do next. The plan had been to get rid of Larry so there was only Madeline and himself.

Larry let her go, turned, and pulled open the shirt of the one who'd been the fist to go. Crowe watched him. He pulled out a couple of the bills and looked up at Crowe.

"I told you."

"That's the money?"

"Look."

"Who are these guys?"

"I don't know."

He was still holding his emptied weapon. The dart worked as fast as it was supposed to and Crowe was glad of that. The last thing she would have known was how stupid it was to link up with someone like Larry. He was Lorenzo's nephew all right, except that Lorenzo was good. But he was a talker, had to make sure you knew how important he was. And now he was talking to visitors too and putting them on to his old buddy Crowe. And telling his nephew about Crowe. That's why the kid had followed him, that's why the girl, that's why all of this.

Crowe lifted his weapon. Larry's eyes followed it, but he wasn't scared. He thought it was just another attempt to get his full attention.

"I don't know where she hooked up with these guys."

The treacherous babble made shooting him easier. An obligation. *Phht.*

Crowe knelt, pushing Larry aside, and took his weapon from his gloved hand and pressed it into Madeline's. Whatever story they made up to explain this mess, Madeline would be the girl who took out three guys.

Unarmed, unencumbered, Crowe started toward the mall. But he stopped before he emerged from the cars, alerted by something, he didn't know what. He dropped from sight and moved swiftly like a Russian dancer backward and then up an alley of cars, weaving between them until he came to a Bronco, top back, open to the sun. He reached in and popped the hood.

He had to get out of here. Get a few miles between him and this goddam city and then everything would be okay. The sound of a helicopter as it came over the building changed everything. He was in the spot he had sworn he would never be in again, but he was calm.

The girl was back there, dead. He was free of that. A car

pulled into an empty space in the next row and Crowe dashed to it, pulled open the passenger door and got in. The woman behind the wheel must have been in her seventies.

"Back out of here, Grandma. We're leaving."

Her mouth opened and she screamed, only no sound came out. She had pushed open the door next to her; the keys were still in her hand. Crowe grabbed the keys and shoved her out the door. She had remembered how to scream before he backed out.

He went at a sedate 20 MPH toward the exit that would take him to a county road that would take him to the interstate that would take him the hell out of this.

Early retirement was what they called it. That's what Crowe intended to do now, what he should have done as soon as that goddam Larry got on his heels—hang it up, beat it south, and sit in the sun with the rest of the retired people.

He should have also taken the money the black guy had taken from Madeline.

Twenty-four

When Lucy telephoned Alma and asked if she could come see her, Alma said sadly that she hadn't planned to go to Michigan City today.

"I just wanted to see you. Talk. Visit. You know."

"Fine. Wonderful." But her tone did not match these exuberant words. "I warn you, though. I have the worst cold."

"You should make a novena."

"I never ask things for myself."

"I'll do it for you."

"Would you?"

"You'll have to tell me what a novena is."

"As soon as you get here."

"Give me directions again."

"That would be easier if you took the bus."

The bus! Lucy was aware that public transportation was still available, but it had become the conveyance of the underclass. Alma lived right on a line; Lucy could get off practically at her door. Lucy realized that the suggestion was perfect. Today would be spent avoiding Crowe, not being anywhere he might expect her to be. She was going underground with the underclass and riding the bus was just the thing.

"When will you come?"

"How long does the bus take?"

Alma's cold made her voice husky and she must be feeling

terrible, but her hospitality was unfeigned now. She would make them a lunch. Did Lucy care for tea? They would have lemon meringue pie for dessert, and no nonsense about diets or calories or anything else. Lucy promised.

She went through the garage and down the alley and to the intersection where she thought there must be a bus stop. There wasn't. Didn't buses run in this neighborhood? Of course they did, bringing in the cleaning ladies in the morning and taking them away again at night. She stood on the curb, undecided. She could call a cab if there was a phone. She could ask where a bus stop was if there was someone to ask. It angered her to feel this helpless. How dependent on automobiles they had become.

She had turned to go back home for her car when a bus appeared. Lucy stepped into the street and waved it down.

"Thank you," she cried, getting on. "How much is the fare?"

She wished she had whispered it. The passengers stared at her as at an intruder. She did whisper when she asked the driver where the bus stop was. He was just pulling into it. Lucy was finding it hard not to feel stupid. She went two-thirds of the way down the aisle where she could claim a whole seat. How hard and uncomfortable it was.

Riding rather than driving permitted her to think. She had been engaged in an unforgiveable act, bringing a paid killer to South Bend and arranging for her own death in a way that would turn suspicion on Warren and Yolande. Now their affair seemed its own punishment. She wanted no revenge. A consequence of suspicion falling on the illicit couple would be to give Max a chance to free himself from Yolande. That was to be Lucy's posthumous gift to him. Before last night, it had been pure benevolence towards Max. Now it was something entirely different, so different she was fleeing the man she had paid to kill her.

Nothing was going to happen today. She could not reach Crowe, but he would be unable to find her. On Fridays she usually spent the afternoon at Service Guild. Crowe had said that he would learn her schedule; he did not want her relating it to him. If he had done his homework, he would know about Service Guild and she felt she had a reasonable chance at safety if she stayed away from there and from every other place where she might conceivably be. She did not think that Crowe would know about Alma.

It was a long uncomfortable ride with the bus rocking in the stretch, lurching into the curb, the driver's foot on the gas pedal tending toward syncopation rather than smoothness. The seat she sat on got harder and harder and finally Lucy was content to stand and grip poles on either side of the aisle and move with the movements of the vehicle. Once she thought of it as skiing, it became tolerable.

Would she have thought of getting in touch with Crowe if she had to ride a bus every day? She was made aware of the level of comfort in her life, the ease of movement due to powerful cars whose seats received and supported the human body. The plastic seats in the bus seemed designed for another species entirely. How many of these passengers were seriously ill, perhaps without knowing, not having the time and luxury to have their bodies regularly monitored? They would soldier on until it was too late for anything but the end, posing no ethical problem. Their lives were only imperfectly in their control, and they knew it. Death was the great imponderable one tried not to think about.

We are all on the same bus, Lucy thought, no matter how we kid ourselves or try to take control. I was so certain of what I wanted when I first talked with Crowe, but all that certainty has fled. Because Max had made love to her?

"You've changed your mind," was the first thing Alma said.

The little woman with the soft dough-like skin met her at the stop and linked her arm in Lucy's and moved her up the sidewalk into a fairly brisk wind.

"Why do you say that?"

"Haven't you?"

"Today was to be the day."

"But you called it off."

"I wasn't able to reach him."

Alma thought about that and then adopted a grim smile, nodding. "You'll be safe with me."

She lived in a one-story duplex, sharing a porch with those who lived in the other half of the stucco house whose low-pitched roof and wide porch with extended eaves gave it a squat and compact look. The light fixture set in the grooved wooden ceiling of the porch was globular, its base black with the carcasses of insects who had found its dim radiance irresistible. The outer door had a bulging screen and the inner door had four narrow windows set in its upper third like exclamation points. The door stuck and Alma put a practiced shoulder into the opening of it. The inside was as simple and comfortable as Alma's soul.

"Is that cinnamon I smell?"

She had heated rolls, thinking Lucy would arrive earlier than she did, and the aroma hung in the house, more sweet and tart when they came into the kitchen. Even more than the rooms through which they had come, the kitchen was spotless and ready for inspection by some imaginary Mother Superior, or maybe just God himself now. Sitting at the kitchen table, with coffee and rolls before them, they talked about the arrangements Lucy had made.

Watching Alma's reaction to what she said gave Lucy for

the first time an estimate of her plan that reached back before the assumptions of the moment and saw them as they would have been seen fifty years ago, a hundred years ago, a thousand years ago, from time immemorial, but deprived of the condescending assumption that we know things all those previous generations did not. The result was that Lucy consciously felt like the post-Christian she was. Warren seemed to think that they believed what their parents, or at least their grandparents, had believed, but they didn't. Not at all. They didn't even know what those beliefs were anymore.

"Have you been praying for me, Alma?"

"I said I would."

"But that was to get me cured."

Alma nodded. "How do you feel?"

"I never did feel badly. Not yet. It's what is to come . . ."

"But it won't. Not now. Of course we all have to die sometime. I'm not asking that you never die."

Lucy said how ironic it was that it was working with prisoners that had opened the way to putting her plan into effect.

"I felt so good about being good. I think I thought those prisoners were less than human, not like us. I found out how much I had in common with them."

Alma spoke of prisoners she had known who did the kind of job Lucy had wanted done.

"I wonder if you knew the one I've dealt with," Lucy said.

"Is his name Crowe?"

Phelps was pulled in several directions as matters developed. The confusion at the mall was total when those in pursuit of the trio had stumbled on the bodies in the parking lot.

"They're all dead," was the first report.

"All three of them?"

"Four."

"There are only three. You've seen the pictures."

He couldn't answer for the police, but his own people had been thoroughly prepared, shown stills and video of Crowe and Larry and the girl.

"The girl's dead. And the young guy."

"Is Crowe there?"

Even as he asked he knew Crowe had slipped away while the police and Phelps's employees counted bodies in the parking lot.

That was why Phelps continued on his way to check on the protection being given Lucy. The man who meant to kill her was still loose, and it had to be assumed that he would do what he had been paid to do.

"No one has shown up," he was told when he checked with Marge.

"She still in there?"

Marge seemed surprised by the question. "Yes."

"Are you sure?"

It seemed best to directly verify that Lucy was still in her well-guarded house. At the door, he punched the button and listened to the chimes within. A minute passed. He activated the chimes once more, but he didn't remain on the front stoop but circled the house. Ashley was seated in a lawn chair beside an outdoor grill that occupied a far corner of the yard. Phelps hit the back doorbell and then strode across the lawn to Ashley who rose to meet him.

"She's not answering the bell."

Ashley shrugged. "She's in there."

"You're sure."

"No one has come out that door since I got here."

Phelps looked at the house and at the attached garage. There was a greenhouse attached to the side of the garage, entered through a door inside the garage. Through the window of that door Phelps saw that Lucy's car was still there.

He went back to the door and pounded on the frame, at the same time bringing out a ring of keys. The door still vibrated with his pounding as he slipped a key into the lock and turned it. He let himself into the house and sensed immediately that she was not here.

"Mrs. Flood," he called, going through the dining room into the living room. He took the stairs two at a time, but he had been right: she was not here.

In the kitchen, he opened the door into the garage. There was her car, no doubt about it. And then he noticed the door at the back of the garage. He went around her car, ducked under an overhanging cabinet and opened the door. It gave onto the alley. Ashley would not have seen anyone leave through this door. Or enter.

The realization hit him hard. The woman targeted to be killed today, the woman his people and the police were guarding, had slipped away.

A situation that had seemed under control wasn't. There were two unknowns. Where was the assassin? Where was his intended victim?

Warren knew enough about hospitals to realize that anyone who moved purposefully was assumed to be on business there. He sailed through the lobby, past the visitors' elevators and continued down a corridor. He hummed and looked thoughtful and had no idea where he would find Max.

Fortunately the place was posted as if for the guidance of idiots. He followed the signs, rose to the 18th floor, still humming, and went in the direction of cardiac surgery. The door of the staff lounge was open, and when he looked in, there was Max, slumped in a chair, his feet out in front of him, listening to an obviously excited Lodge.

"Warren!" Max said in surprise. "How in hell did you get up here?"

Lodge scrambled to his feet and took Warren's hand. He wore an idiot's grin.

"Max just told me she changed her mind. Thank God. She can be helped, you know. She wouldn't accept that, but it's true."

Max rose too and took hold of Lodge's upper arm.

"Why don't you take Warren down to the cafeteria?"

"I'm here to see you."

Max bared a hairy wrist and consulted a watch that looked as if it told the time of four continents. "I'm due back in surgery, Warren. It'll have to wait. Go have a cup of coffee with Dr. Lodge."

"You were at my house last night."

Lodge said, "I asked him to go, to add his advice to mine. And it worked."

"What the hell are you talking about?"

"That's why you have to talk to Lodge, Warren."

Max clapped him on the back, and Warren stepped away, not wanting to be touched by the man who had wormed himself between Warren and his wife.

A nurse dressed like Max came and began to chatter to him, consulting a metal clipboard, and then the two of them left the lounge. Warren allowed himself to be led away by Lodge.

"I don't trust that guy," Warren muttered.

"Oh, he's the best heart man we have."

They rode down in silence. When they were seated with paper cups of coffee, Lodge unburdened himself.

"I agonized about not going to you, but we are so hemmed in now. The most obvious things, or things which once were obvious, have become minefields. Legally."

"I'm a lawyer."

"Then you know. Of course I wanted to tell you immediately, if only to get you to add your voice to mine and persuade her to undergo treatment. People simply won't believe the strides we have made in the treatment of cancer, even the advanced cases."

"Cancer?"

Lodge nodded, rambling as if they had already discussed Lucy's illness, the melanoma that had seemed cured, her recent appointment. Warren knew nothing of melanoma. Listening to Lodge, he was filled with the stunned feeling that he knew less of his wife than Lodge and Max and God knew how many others. Lodge was babbling about the ethics panel and its discussion.

"How sick is she?"

Abruptly, Lodge's exuberance was gone. "I won't arouse false hopes. It is terminal."

Warren's silence made Lodge talkative again. Lucy with cancer, Lucy under sentence of death, Lucy keeping this a secret from him. The last realization was even worse than the others. She had deliberately excluded him from this radical alteration in her life. She preferred to face death alone, with only physicians and surgeons in on the secret. Lodge seemed eager to elicit some sign of approval from Warren, but Warren was in no position to help him. Lodge apparently thought he had learned all these things despite the conspiracy to keep them from him.

"Let me get you a hot coffee."

Warren looked at the paper cup with its reinforced rim, its little handle that had been embedded in its side, at the dark and now cool contents. He shook his head and pushed back from the table.

"I can't tell you what a relief it is to talk with you about this finally."

Warren nodded.

"I was afraid she would take her own life."

It was with those words clattering around in his mind that Warren walked from the restaurant and down the corridor and through the lobby and out to the parking lot where he got behind the wheel of his car and burst into tears.

Warren's persistent phone calls had put Yolande on edge. She had been on edge since their talk on the club verandah when he had told her that Lucy had made arrangements to have him killed and that Yolande too was in danger. That was absurd. But it was an absurdity difficult to dismiss once you admitted that Warren was in danger. Max's assumption that she had received bad medical news from Lodge, a tender moment when she assured him she was perfectly healthy, provided Lucy's grim motivation. She had been told she was seriously ill and her first reaction was to take revenge on Warren. Because he was unfaithful. And of course that included her.

This cleared her mind. She found it difficult now to believe that she had ever felt the least attraction for Warren Flood. It was unthinkable that she should jeopardize her marriage to Max for a few stolen moments with a man like Warren.

He was nothing but a big kid, really. He hadn't grown up. He was supposed to be an okay lawyer, but he did not rank in his profession as Max ranked in his.

But it was Warren's repeated statement that he had dealt with the threat posed by Lucy's hiring an assassin that filled her mind. He had himself met with the gunman, but he would not tell her what had gone on. Would he have convinced them to make Lucy the target? And if Lucy, Max too?

My God. That had to be it. That's why he wouldn't tell her

the details. That was why he said she would be surprised.

Yolande flew down the stairs, lost her footing as she came to the landing and bounced down the rest of the steps on the seat of her jeans. In the hallway, she looked at the phone. She snatched it up and dialed Warren's office.

"Mr. Flood," she said, when a girl answered by reciting the name of the firm.

"Thank you for calling Mitchell, Forrest and Barnum."

Another ringing and then the voice Yolande recognized as that of Warren's secretary.

"This is Mrs. Flood," she said. "Is Warren in?"

"Oh hi. No, he isn't."

"When did he get in this morning?"

"He hasn't been in yet."

"Thank you."

"I'll tell him you called."

Yolande went into the garage, got into her car, started it and very nearly backed up before she remembered to raise the garage door. And then she was on her way to the hospital.

Warren lifted his face from his arms braced by his grip on the top of the steering wheel. He took a deep breath. It had been stupid to come here and confront Max. What had he been thinking of? That being with Max when it happened, if it happened, would make him an unlikely suspect? After the scene in the surgeons' lounge he would be the first one thought of if anything happened to Max.

He picked up his phone, stared at it, put it down. He turned on the radio, WCCM, perpetual news. A massacre at the mall was being breathlessly reported. Two black youths, and a white couple, preliminary indications were that the white woman had killed the three others and had in turn been killed by some kind of dart.

Warren thought of the oasis on the toll road. He thought of the mousy girl and the young man with the bright shifty eyes, his hair gathered into a ponytail. Was it them? And then the mention of money at the scene, an envelope of one-hundred-dollar bills. His money. It was gone for good and he hadn't got what he'd paid for.

He felt relief. Thank God. To hell with the money. There was no way it could be traced to him. Warren felt cleansed, no longer in danger. Even a failed attempt to have Max harmed would have been the end of his career.

Nothing had happened between Max and Lucy, he assured himself. Nothing happened.

He looked across the lot to the revolving door of the hospital. It was oversized and moved slowly, the better to permit released patients to be wheeled through and to their cars. Max had returned to surgery, but eventually he would be done. The thing to do was to be waiting for him and erase the memory of the earlier confrontation. He might even tell Max about himself and Yolande.

It seemed an inspiration. Deflating Max had its attractions and it wasn't an actionable offense. He picked up his phone and called his office.

"You must be wondering what happened to me."

"You've missed two appointments."

"You rescheduled them?"

"Yes. Will you be in?"

"I can't seem to shake this flu."

A palpably skeptical silence oozed along the line.

"Mrs. Flood called."

"When was that?"

"A few minutes ago."

"Any message?"

"No."

He hung up and dialed Yolande but received no answer. There was a tapping on his window, and he looked up to find Yolande standing beside the car. He rolled down the window, and she brought a pistol up until its barrel was only inches from his eyes.

"Where the hell would she go?" Marge asked and Phelps looked at her. Where would a needle go in a haystack? Her husband? No way. Max Kramer? That made more sense, not much more, but Phelps couldn't think of anything better.

"Come on," he called to Marge and started back to his van.

"You're relieving me?"

"Come on!"

From the van he let the police know that Lucy was gone.

"Gone where?"

"Ask the detail you had watching her house."

"Where we going?" Marge asked.

"For a ride." He did not want to explain that they were following a wild hunch. The closer he got to the hospital the sillier it seemed. "Good morning, Doctor, sorry to interrupt you in the middle of brain surgery, but I wonder if another man's wife dropped by to see you."

He put on the police frequency and was not surprised to hear that they had no idea where Crowe was.

Twenty-five

Crowe had reached the moment of truth and he knew it. He had come within an ace of losing it all because of his actions, explained by an attraction to Madeline that made no sense. Now Madeline was gone and he was free again. And in maximum danger. He had to get rid of this car and get another. No, the first thing was to be calm, drive slowly, not call attention to himself.

He entered the traffic on Cleveland and then, because the light permitted it, turned left on Highway 23 toward downtown. The road became two lanes, but there were cars in front of him as well as behind, making him just another driver on a busy road. Except that the woman who owned this car, if she had not been injured when he shoved her out the door, would be sounding the alarm and the license plate number and model of car would go out to all patrol cars. Still, it would take time. He was betting on the woman's being too shaken up to know what to do, at least immediately. He thought of her struggling to her feet and hobbling toward the mall . . .

He frowned. There was something about that old woman, the look on her face . . .

He had been thinking of her for a minute before he realized it. Of course. The woman they had called Alma Mater. They kidded about her, about the way she treated them as if all the lies they told were true. Everyone in Michigan City had been wrongfully accused and unjustly condemned. Alma be-

197

lieved it. Or acted as if she did. Crowe figured she was dumber than most of them, but he learned that wasn't it. It wasn't the past Alma had been interested in, but now, what your life could be from now on. When he would sit talking to her, he would promise that his life would be different and they would plan how he would go about it once he got out. It was Alma's advice that he had followed in being a model parolee. The rest of the plan was that he should learn a trade, go to work, settle down. But Crowe had simply been clearing the slate so that he could carry out his own plan, the one he had formulated listening to Lorenzo White.

Now that his trip to South Bend had ended in disaster, Crowe suddenly wanted to see Alma again, wanted the reassurance of her trust and faith in him. He'd find a phone directory and look up her address.

At Eddy, again because the light permitted it, he turned south. The traffic was thinner on this city street and he felt exposed. As soon as he could, he turned west and in a few blocks found himself in a hospital complex. There would be lots of phones there. The sight of the lot filled with cars brought a smile to his lips. He could have cried out in relief.

He pulled into the physicians' lot and eased the car into an empty space. Stepping from the car and looking around, he felt he had come full circle. It was in the airport parking lot that things had started to go wrong. They were going to go *right* from now on. He got the door of a nondescript but expensive car open and popped the lid. He was leaning over the motor when he heard the voices behind him.

He froze. And listened. The woman's voice became a screech and the man's a roar of anger. Crowe turned and saw a couple struggling. They were fighting over a gun! Crowe closed the hood of the car and circled around toward the quarreling couple. He came swiftly up behind the woman and pinned her arms to her side and pulled her back. The gun fell from her hand and the man, startled by Crowe's arrival, now stared dumbly at the gun. Crowe felt a sharp pain in his shin when the struggling woman brought her heel swiftly back. He flung her aside and picked up the gun.

"Crowe," the man said. "You're Crowe." There was terror in his eyes.

That settled it. Crowe put the gun on him, reached for the woman's arm and hauled her to her feet. Which one of these idiots should he have drive? He decided on the woman. She was trying to kick him again, and he had to twist her arm up her back. The man who recognized him looked too scared to drive.

He opened the driver door and pushed her in. "Get in back," he told the man.

He scrambled to do so, and Crowe got into the passenger seat, sitting sideways, so he could see them both. The key was in the ignition.

"Drive."

"You go to hell."

"Yolande! For God's sake, do what he says."

The woman turned to look at him, then looked at Crowe. "Who are you?"

"The bogeyman."

She turned away and pressed down on the door handle. He caught her behind the ear with the barrel of the gun, and she fell forward, her head bouncing off the window. He looked at the man in the back seat.

"Listen. We are going to put her in the back seat and you are going to drive."

"I'll help you with Yolande, but I can't drive."

Yolande. Crowe said nothing until they had the woman's limp body in the back seat. The man hesitated, and written all over his face was the wish that he had guts enough to make a run for it.

"How do you know who I am?"

"I don't!"

"You used my name."

"I didn't. I swear I didn't."

"You called her Yolande."

He didn't know what to say to that. But Crowe had it now anyway. The woman, Mrs. Flood, had tried to pass herself off as Yolande. Yolande was the woman her husband was fooling around with. And this was Warren.

"Get behind the wheel, Warren."

He got behind the wheel as some men go willingly to their death. Crowe got in beside him and pulled the door closed. "See that row of outdoor phones? Pull over there." Warren drove and pulled up close. With the gun trained on Warren, Crowe pulled the phone book on the cable to the window. The light from over the phone gave him enough illumination. He flipped pages, then scribbled down the address.

"Drive." Crowe gave Warren the address.

It didn't matter that he had told Warren where they were going. It didn't matter at all. He and Yolande were two loose ends to be taken care of before he talked to Alma and figured out how to get out of town and on the way to anonymity and freedom. Or maybe he would stay with Alma awhile. The more he thought of her, the more she seemed like the mother he had never known, an all forgiving, sympathetic ally.

In the midst of the confusion came the excited call from security at St. Joseph Medical Center about a three-way quarrel in the parking lot. Phelps smiled at the profane reaction to what was obviously considered a comic interruption.

The detectives assigned to Max Kramer were asked what was going on.

"In the parking lot?" Incredulity.

"Where's Dr. Kramer?"

"I can see him from where I stand."

"Keep it that way."

Phelps told Marge to head for the hospital and she asked if he thought the doctor was still in danger.

"I don't know."

Warren Flood was not in his office, nor had he been heard from for some time. Did they expect him in?

"Would you care to make an appointment?"

"Some other time."

Phelps checked on Yolande Kramer as well and learned that she had left her house.

"Where is she now?"

"Check with her husband. She parked in the visitors' lot of the hospital about half an hour ago."

"Is she inside the hospital?"

"She went in the front entrance." The smug tone of his operative's report angered Phelps.

"Why didn't you follow her?"

"I figure she's got to come back for her car."

"Is it still there?"

"I have it under surveillance."

That was arguably the smart decision. There were several exits from the hospital that Yolande Kramer could take to get back to her car. And Marge could easily get lost inside the medical center.

"Good. Some kind of argument was reported in the physicians' parking lot."

"That's around back."

Beside him, Marge said nothing, but he could hear

through the silence her wonder at what they were doing. They were floundering, that's what they were doing. The whole damned operation had failed, every subject had somehow managed to disappear and the assassin too. What else could he do but the stupid thing they were doing? It seemed somewhat less stupid to suggest that the police put out an all points bulletin on the automobiles of Warren Flood and Yolande Kramer.

Crowe liked the feel of the gun he had taken from Yolande Kramer. It was obviously well taken care of; it would no doubt be registered, the defensive weapon of a law abiding citizen, the sort of gun that by and large ended up in the hands of someone like himself. He wanted to ask Warren why the woman had come after him with a gun, if that is what had happened. Neither one seemed the type to be struggling over a hand weapon in a hospital parking lot.

"Is that loaded?" Warren asked.

For answer, Crowe pointed the gun at the ceiling of the car and pulled the trigger. Warren nearly lost control of the car at the sound of the shot. Above Crowe's head a fresh hole gave a jagged view of the sky. Crowe grabbed the wheel and steadied the car. That had been a stupid trick, worthy of Larry, the poor sonofabitch. He did not want to think of Madeline, part of the grisly pile of bodies, the gun held in her lifeless hand. He would use this gun to silence Warren and the woman in the back seat. Her painful groan became audible. Crowe reached over the seat and gave her another whack with her revolver.

He should get rid of them before reaching Alma's house, but the route they were on was no place to do the job. Shooting a hole in the ceiling of a moving vehicle might have drawn unwelcome attention, but having Warren pull over to the curb so he could shoot them both was out. It was a dilemma. If he had Warren drive him right to Alma's door, Alma would be a witness of the double killing, and that would jeopardize her, and he didn't want to do that. She had become the only one in the world he could trust and he did not want to lose the total sympathy she had shown him in the past. After all, she had never witnessed any of the deeds he was accused of, but those were deeds far less serious than those that hung over him now.

He ran his finger along the warm barrel of the gun. And noticed the car phone. He picked it up and punched out the number of Alma's phone. Nothing happened.

"Doesn't this thing work?"

"Did you dial?"

"You heard me."

"Press enter."

He did and the phone began to ring. When she answered, he said, "Alma?"

"Just a minute."

While he waited for Alma he accepted the fact that she was not alone. There was another woman there. At least. For all he knew he was driving toward a house full of ladies and he doubted that any other woman would be as unforgiving as Alma.

"Yes."

"This is Philip Crowe."

"Well, speak of the devil."

"What do you mean?"

"I had just mentioned your name."

"Why?"

She didn't answer right away, and he felt trust drain from him. The Alma he remembered must be an imaginary creature, he thought grimly. The real Alma was thinking up a lie to tell him. Had the police talked to her? Was the woman with her a cop?

"Philip, where are you?"

"I'm coming to see you."

"Oh good! When?"

He hung up; they must be nearly there. Why would she ask when he was coming if she didn't mean to have the police waiting for him? Crowe was certain that the whole world was now searching for him. All his enemies would soon converge on him. He had dreaded the thought of going back to prison, but now he feared he would never get there. He was being hunted down and it would be easier to settle matters now.

Alma turned to Lucy. "You'll never guess who that was."

"I recognized his voice." Not at the time, not when she answered the phone, but while Alma was speaking. The former nun seemed delighted by the surprising call.

"Everything happens for a reason," she assured Lucy.

Was religious faith really all that different? Most people assumed that their lives made sense, that things hang together, that bad luck was some kind of warning or punishment, not just something that happened to you. Lucy's first reaction to the news that Crowe was coming here to Alma's was to leave. She had come here to avoid him and now he had found her. But she was avoiding him because she had been unable to tell him she no longer wanted him to do what she had hired him for. Now she could tell him face to face, quelling any anger by telling him he could keep the money. What did money matter? What Dr. Lodge had told her still loomed over her, no matter Alma's prayers to Our Lady of Fatima. But Lucy was determined now to go on living under sentence of death—like everyone else.

"How did he know I was here?"

A little frown passed over Alma's brow. "Does he know?"

"Why else is he coming?"

Too late she realized that she had deprived Alma of much of her delight at the phone call from Philip Crowe. She saw him as a lost sheep returning to the fold, one of her special cares, coming to her now in a moment of need. They had talked about Lucy's arrangement with Crowe, of the assassin's visit to South Bend. And the radio had been giving them news Alma was certain related to Crowe. The slaughter in the parking lot of the mall had filled the former nun with dread. But it was the effect on Crowe of what had happened rather than the victims found lying in the parking lot that Alma concentrated on.

"Do you think he was responsible?"

"You mean killed them? Oh no. You heard the report. But now they are hunting for him."

Would Alma protect the assassin, give him refuge, attempt to persuade him to face up to whatever he had done? Just asking those questions was to know their answer. Lucy wanted to see the man with whom she had been dealing. What would he look like? Lorenzo had been rendered harmless in prison and his dreadful stories about what he had done had an aura of make believe about them. They had happened, if they had happened, at another time, somewhere else. They never seemed fully real. Was she now to meet the assassin she had hired face to face, here and now, the hunted rather than the hunter?

Alma had been standing near a window that gave a view of the street. She pulled back the curtain, then let it drop and headed for the kitchen.

"He's going around back."

An alley ran behind the houses and Alma's garage was approached from the alley. She went out onto the back porch but Lucy remained inside, behind the screen door, watching. The car pulled in.

The passenger door opened and a spare tallish man ducked out. He looked toward Alma and his expression did not change but something in the shift of his upper body suggested pleasure and relief at the sight of her. He dipped down and looked into the car. The driver door opened and a man emerged, bent over, head bowed. Lucy pushed through the door and joined Alma.

The man who must be Crowe had pulled open the back door of the car and the driver, in response to an order, opened the opposite door. Crowe reached in and began to pull something from the back seat. Before the driver had crept through the back seat, carrying his end of the burden, it became clear what they were carrying. And that the other man was Warren.

"Yolande!" Lucy cried, and started down the steps.

Alma caught at her arm and was pulled along as Lucy went toward the car. Crowe had turned when she cried out Yolande's name.

"It's all right," Alma called out. "It's all right, Philip."

He released his grip on Yolande's ankles, and they dropped to the ground.

"Bring her inside," Alma urged.

Crowe faced them now and he was holding a gun. It seemed to complete his persona. What is an assassin without a weapon? But it made him seem more pathetic than menacing. The murderous gunman had come scuttling to Alma when his plans began to fall apart.

"Put that away," Lucy said, advancing on him with Alma hurrying along beside her. "I've changed my mind. There's no need for that."

But he was raising the gun, as if Lucy represented danger. She permitted Alma to stop her.

"I am Lucy Flood. We've spoken on the phone . . ."

The gun continued to lift, slowly, deliberately, as if it was for this that he had come and Lucy was filled with the realization that she had set something in motion she could not simply stop with a word. He was aiming at her. He seemed determined to do what she had hired him to do no matter what she said.

Before the gun went off, Alma gave Lucy a push that spun her off balance, and she fell to her knees on the lawn. To her right, there was a voice crying out in pain. And Lucy saw Alma's knees buckle as she sank to the ground, a stunned expression on her face, blood gushing from a dreadful wound in her throat. Lucy scrambled toward her, wanting to take her in her arms, but Alma slumped away.

Lucy turned toward Crowe. But the gunman was no longer standing there with the pathetic authority of that gun in his hand. Warren had grasped him from behind and was wrestling him back toward the car. He made a turning twisting motion and brought the gunman's head against the side of the car. This stunned Crowe. Then Warren grabbed him by the hair and began to beat his head against the car. Lucy got to her feet, looked with horror at the lifeless body of Alma and then knelt beside her.

The sound of a siren brought Warren to his senses, and he stopped banging Crowe's head against the car. He had kicked the gun away, into the hedge bordering the yard. Now he shoved Crowe into the still open back door of the car and slammed it shut. Yolande, bedraggled, her hair fallen forward over her face, had gotten into a sitting position. Fear and relief succeeded one another on her face and then came admiration at what Warren had done.

Warren turned toward Lucy, kneeling like a religious

figure beside the fallen body of the woman Crowe had shot when she pushed Lucy aside and came into the range of fire. Lucy looked back at him, tears running down her face, the picture of grief.

"Warren!" Yolande called out to him.

He looked down at her and then again up the walk where Lucy gathered the lifeless woman into her arms. Warren went slowly to his wife and helped her attend to the woman who had saved her life.